The McKenna Legacy...
A Legacy of Love

To my darling grandchildren,

I leave you my love and more. Within thirty-three days of your thirty-third birthday—enough time to know what you are about—you will have in your grasp a legacy of which your dreams are made. Dreams are not always tangible things, but more often are born in the heart. Act selflessly in another's behalf, and my legacy will be yours.

Your loving grandmother,
Moira McKenna

P.S. Use any other inheritance from me wisely and only for good, lest you destroy yourself or those you love.

Dear Harlequin Intrigue Reader,

May holds more mayhem for you in this action-packed month of terrific titles.

Patricia Rosemoor revisits her popular series THE McKENNA LEGACY in this first of a two-book miniseries. Irishman Curran McKenna has a gift for gentling horses—and the ladies. But Thoroughbred horse owner Jane Grantham refuses to be tamed—especially when she is guarding not only her heart, but secrets that could turn deadly. Will she succumb to this *Mysterious Stranger*?

Bestselling author Joanna Wayne delivers the final book in our MORIAH'S LANDING in-line continuity series. In *Behind the Veil*, we finally meet the brooding recluse Dr. David Bryson. Haunted for years by his fiancée's death, he meets a new woman in town who wants to teach him how to love again. But when she is targeted as a killer's next victim, David will use any means necessary to make sure that history doesn't repeat itself.

The Bride and the Mercenary continues Harper Allen's suspenseful miniseries THE AVENGERS. For two years Ainslie O'Connor believed that the man she'd passionately loved—Seamus Malone—was dead. But then she arrives at her own society wedding, only to find that her dead lover is still alive! Will Seamus's memory return in time to save them both?

And finally, we are thrilled to introduce a brand-new author—Lisa Childs. You won't want to miss her very first book *Return of the Lawman*—with so many twists and turns, it will keep you guessing…and looking for more great stories from her!

Happy reading,

Denise O'Sullivan
Associate Senior Editor
Harlequin Intrigue

MYSTERIOUS STRANGER
PATRICIA ROSEMOOR

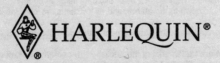

TORONTO • NEW YORK • LONDON
AMSTERDAM • PARIS • SYDNEY • HAMBURG
STOCKHOLM • ATHENS • TOKYO • MILAN • MADRID
PRAGUE • WARSAW • BUDAPEST • AUCKLAND

ISBN 0-373-22661-6

MYSTERIOUS STRANGER

Copyright © 2002 by Patricia Pinianski

Visit us at www.eHarlequin.com

Printed in U.S.A.

ABOUT THE AUTHOR

To research her novels, Patricia Rosemoor is willing to swim with dolphins, round up mustangs or howl with wolves…"Whatever it takes to write a credible tale." She's the author of contemporary, historical and paranormal romances, but her first love has always been romantic suspense. She won both a *Romantic Times* Career Achievement Award in Series Romantic Suspense and a Reviewer's Choice Award for one of her Harlequin Intrigue novels. She's written more than thirty Harlequin Intrigue books and is now writing for Harlequin Blaze. She lives in Chicago with her husband, Edward, and their three cats.

She would love to know what you think of this story. Write to Patricia Rosemoor at P.O. Box 578297, Chicago, IL 60657-8297 or via e-mail at Patricia@PatriciaRosemoor.com, and visit her Web site at http://PatriciaRosemoor.com.

Books by Patricia Rosemoor

HARLEQUIN INTRIGUE

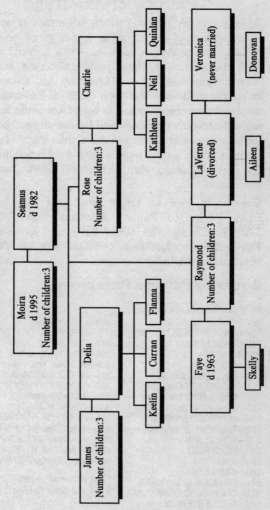

McKENNA FAMILY TREE

- Descendants of MOIRA KELLY McKENNA

Moira d 1995
Number of children: 3

Seamus d 1982

James
Number of children: 3

Rose
Number of children: 3

Charlie

Delia

Raymond
Number of children: 3

Keelin

Curran

Flanna

Kathleen

Neil

Quinlan

Veronica
(never married)

LaVerne
(divorced)

Faye d 1963

Skelly

Aileen

Donovan

CAST OF CHARACTERS

Curran McKenna—The Irish horse trainer with a special gift comes to Kentucky to gentle a traumatized Thoroughbred and finds he needs to do the same with the stallion's owner.

Jane (Sheena) Grantham—The beautiful farm manager is seething with guilt over her failure to protect her beloved horse and herself from a pipe-wielding attacker.

Finn mac Cumhail—The crazed Thoroughbred won't let anyone near him except Jane.

Gavin Shaw—Jane's former horse trainer who has disappeared was supposed to help get the Grantham farm out of debt.

Ned Flaherty—Curran's new assistant seems too interested in what's going on at Grantham Acres.

Mukhtar Saladin—The Saudi horse owner is intent on his stallion, Stonehenge, winning the Thoroughbred Millions.

Holt Easterling—The British trainer who works for Saladin says he'll do whatever he must to make sure that Stonehenge wins.

Timothy Brady—Holt's assistant used to work for Gavin and knows what happened to Jane and Finn.

Phyllis Singleton-Volmer—The society woman and Thoroughbred owner sees Mukhtar Saladin as husband number three.

Linda, you always have the most devious mind and can turn seemingly innocent locations into something dangerous.

Prologue

A scream woke her.

Not human, she realized, pushing herself up out of a deep sleep.

"What's that?"

The answering whisper came from the rising wind. She was alone.

Moonlight shimmered through the window and over the rumpled quilt that offered comfort against the chill spring night. Another scream, equine, a fusion of fear and fury, drove her up from the bed. She recognized the source.

Heart beating madly, she choked out, "Finn mac Cumhail!"

The damp cold attacked her bare feet, seeped through the long cotton nightgown embracing her full hips and tangling around her thighs as if to trip her. Somehow she bolted through the unfamiliar and darkened kitchen without bumping into anything. In the mudroom, she slid her feet into a pair of muck-covered boots.

Then it was out to the night and into the barn. The handful of stabled horses moved about restlessly. Complaining. But no Finn in his stall. Another squeal came from behind the building. She flew outside and into the pasture that topped the bluff, where fingers of mist rose from the Hudson River below.

Not that the rising fog prevented her from being faced with a horror that she could hardly grasp.

Tied to the fence, the terrified stallion reared to defend himself against the human who wielded a deadly length of pipe. If the Thoroughbred's legs were broken—the obvious intent—his death would be assured.

"Stop!" she screamed.

He did halt for a moment to glance back, and the only way she could describe him with the moon-gleam silvering his distorted features was deranged. As crazed as the horse who twisted and turned from the lead that secured him to the fence post.

What could cause such desperation?

Anguish tore through her heart as she rushed to stop this desecration, for his shaky hand was already lifting for another strike. He was drunk—she noted how he lurched as he tried to take aim.

Fearing for the stallion, she didn't hesitate to position herself between the powerful chestnut and him. "Enough!"

Too late. Already on its trajectory, the pipe contacted not the horse's leg, but hers. A sharp crack... waves of nauseating pain engulfed her...sent her reeling to the ground. Her strangled cry of disbelief and agony joined with Finn's outraged squeal.

The stallion lunged for him, then, teeth bared, as if to protect her, and the pipe came down. Finn's beautiful velvet nose split like a ripe fruit. Blood sprayed black against the silver light. And closer now, she could see several other wounds on his shoulder and foreleg, all open and weeping.

Tears sprang to her eyes.

"You won't get away with this!" she cried, her heart already broken. "You're a ruined man! No one will ever let you near a horse again!"

It was then he turned on her, his features twisted into a grotesque mask, and she realized that he couldn't—*wouldn't*—allow her to tell the tale.

Fear snaked up into her throat.

"Stay away from me!" she choked out, scrabbling back toward the bluff.

Pipe raised and aimed at her, he advanced.

Frantic for a way out, she looked around wildly for some makeshift weapon that she could use to defend herself. Her gaze lit on the farm tool propped against a fence post—the only ray of hope that she might hold him off and save both herself and Finn.

Rolling out of his path, she lunged for the pitchfork and clumsily hefted its awkward weight to keep him away from her.

And then, in a flash, the horror multiplied...

Chapter One

Grantham Acres spread out before them, not unlike a picture-perfect postcard.

Rolling grassy hills neatly surrounded by four-board, white fence and live oak. Grazing Thoroughbred mares with colts and fillies at their sides. And amidst it all, a magnificent house of the Federal style with double pillars that rose on either side of the front door—a splash of blinding white against the surrounding greens.

Curran McKenna stopped the rental car at the top of a rise to take it all in.

"A piece of the old sod, isn't it," Ned Flaherty said from the passenger seat.

Indeed, Curran thought, the Kentucky bluegrass drew its color from an earth rich with lime, which made the connection back to the green hills of Ireland.

He looked to his assistant, middle-aged and comfortable in his country tweeds. "Surely you're not homesick already, and us gone only a day."

"Just a bit more comfortable in this strange land, filled with a stranger people who insist on driving on the wrong side of the road," Ned groused, furrowing his forehead so his thick, wild reddish-brown eyebrows drew together.

Curran laughed. Americans were a faster-paced, more serious, less talkative people than the Irish. Other than that, he didn't see much difference. People were people—good, bad, indifferent. Every country had its mix.

Besides, they weren't here to socialize but on a mission of mercy.

Curran continued toward the front entrance to the estate. Hard to believe that at the heart of this beauty lay something dark enough to sadden the soul.

Finn mac Cumhail gone mad—Curran could hardly fathom it.

What could have happened to the magnificent creature he'd gentled into the racing circuit three years before?

A long drive swept them up toward the house. The grounds were lushly landscaped, the flower beds separated from the blacktop by low limestone walls similar to those found in the Irish countryside.

Only when they stopped in the circular driveway before the front door did Curran notice the signs of wear that told him the house needed tending. He slid out from behind the driver's seat and took a better look around at the house and one of the barns. Peeling paint and rotting wood were always a problem back home where most every day was soft with rain. But he was surprised to see any signs of neglect here under such a glorious sun and on such a magnificent property.

The front door opened and an attractive older woman dressed in denims and a knit polo shirt

stepped outside with a friendly wave. "You must be
Mr. McKenna."

"And you must be Jane Grantham."

"I'm Belle. Jane is my granddaughter."

A youthful grandmother, Curran thought, noting
the silver wings in the woman's short, light brown
hair. His own grandmother Moira McKenna, God
bless her soul, hadn't had a thing on this woman in
that department.

He shook her hand and introduced Ned, who was
immediately at his best. "If you're a grandmother,
then Miss Jane must be barely out of the school-
room."

Belle laughed. "You're a charmer."

But before Ned could counter, a shrill cry split the
air.

"Finn?"

"I'm afraid so. Jane is obsessed with that horse.
She can't leave him alone for a day. And unfortunately, he doesn't appreciate her efforts."

"What happened? To craze him, I mean."

Belle appeared stricken. She shook her head. "I
don't know. Some kind of terrible accident. That's
all Jane would say."

"Then it's off to find out," Curran said, instincts
already humming.

He started off in the direction of the disturbance.

"No, wait! Um, Mr. McKenna…"

He stopped and turned to face her. "Curran."

"Curran, Jane isn't expecting you."

"But she's the one who wrote me."

"No. *I* wrote you on her letterhead and signed her
name. I thought you would be more convinced if the

plea came from the farm manager. I meant to tell her, I really did. I just couldn't find the words.''

Sensing her desperation, Curran chose not to make an issue of the deception. "I am Irish, so I'll not be having trouble with words," he said instead.

He was here now. And he was obviously needed. No need to distress her further.

Seeming a bit relieved, she nodded. "I hope you have the right ones, then. I haven't been able to get through to Jane. No trainer in this area will take on Finn. A few have tried...but they all say he needs to be..." She swallowed hard and went on. "Jane is determined to fix Finn herself, as if she is somehow to blame. But how can she fix him, when she can't even fix herself?''

Wondering what she meant by the last, Curran said, "I'll be keeping that in mind, then. I assume you do have a place for us to stay the night?"

"Yes, of course," Belle said, finding a smile. "A very comfortable guest house for you, as promised, and cozy quarters for your assistant in the renovated stable that also houses the farm office."

Curran turned to Ned. "Perhaps you could settle us in?" He wanted to appraise the situation alone.

"Of course."

"If you just drive around that way," Belle told Ned, "you'll come to the guest house, and behind that the stables with your quarters."

"Good enough."

Ned hopped behind the wheel even as they all heard further commotion from Finn. Curran quickly took his leave.

Rounding the house, he saw the barn fronted by a round paddock. He stopped in the shadows opposite, so that he could have a look without being seen himself.

A great flash of deep red caught his attention.

Finn, agitated.

The source of the stallion's irritation had her back to him. Taller than average, she had curvy, childbearing hips, Curran noticed. Her shoulder-length curls of medium brown were struck with gold.

He willed her to turn, to face him, so that he could get the full picture.

But Jane Grantham's concentration was focused on getting a halter on the stallion. She had no idea that she was being watched.

She and Finn were playing a serious game of advance and retreat, for he was having none of the leathers she offered. Each time she lifted the halter toward his head, Finn would roll his eyes, stomp his hooves and squeal in protest, then dart away from her.

Curran watched intently, noting the woman's strange gait as she turned with and approached the horse. Perhaps part of the problem, he thought, already analyzing. Finn was in a fragile mental state caused by an accident of some sort. Jane's odd gait might signal danger and be enough to alarm him further.

Five minutes went by. Ten. And yet she got no closer to her goal.

Fifteen.

Tiring of the futility, Curran was about to announce himself, when the Grantham woman almost had the stallion, the halter creeping inches over his nose. But at the last moment, Finn threw up his head and wheeled around, his powerful shoulder grazing her.

Though the contact appeared minimal, she couldn't keep her balance and spun to the ground.

Curran flew toward the paddock, hearing her soft cries split the air.

Sobs that gave way to keening.

Not the sound of physical hurt, but something that went deeper. More intimate.

Something that kept him silent.

He drew close enough to see her huddled on the ground, folded in on herself, rocking, crying as though her heart was breaking.

Or perhaps it had already been broken, he mused.

Her soft wail split his chest and curled around his own heart, and for a moment, stole his very breath.

An eye to Finn told him the stallion was equally bothered by her keening. But rather than retreating to a far corner of the paddock as Curran expected him to do, he approached the Grantham woman, though on an oblique angle, nearly walking past before turning to eye her.

That was when Curran got a good look at the horrifying scars that now marred the chestnut's beauty.

What the hell had happened to him? Curran wondered.

Then Finn did the most amazing thing.

The stallion moved in until his neck hung directly over her curled, shaking body. Dipping his head, the horse snorted in her hair and chewed at it a moment before lifting his head.

Finn stood there, then. Quiet. Unmoving. Protective.

Looking for all the world like an equine body-guard.

A force vibrated between horse and human so strongly that Curran felt it like a physical blow. He concentrated, psychically eavesdropped, tried to grasp the bond, to make it his own so that he could read it, and for his trouble was plunged into a waking void.

For a moment, the dark consumed him, as did the negative energy that quaked through him with a life of its own.

Fear...hatred...horror...

He felt them all.

But from whom? The horse? Or the woman?

A flash of something solid hurtling toward him through the haze of his mind...

A startled Curran popped back into the moment.

All was the same. Horse and human inexorably connected by some horror he could not yet fathom. He backed off, unwilling to break their bond.

Besides, he needed time alone to gather his thoughts. To figure out what had just happened.

To best decide how to approach not only the stallion, but the woman herself.

TAKING A DEEP BREATH to help her calm down, Jane grew aware of the big, warm body protecting hers.

"Ah, Finn, we make a fine pair, don't we."

She reached out to touch one of his scars. Her fingertips barely brushed him. His flesh quivered and he stepped back with a nervous whinny.

She let her hand drop.

"Don't worry. Enough for today. For both of us."

Then she had to figure out how to get back up off

the ground. Nearly three months since the surgery
and still she hadn't mastered some of the simplest
movements that she had once taken for granted.

Awkwardly, she rolled to her good knee, and placing her palms flat against the earth, pushed up and
staggered to her feet. Somehow, the ground felt different beneath the left one. The knee didn't tolerate
the dips and rises. So often, she stepped wrong,
which could mean agony for hours or even days.
Luckily, the fall hadn't kicked up the pain.

Moving to the fence, she was irritated that her gait
had been further affected.

Damn limp! she groused to herself as she grabbed
her cane. When would she be free of it?

"Come, Finn, it's time to go inside," she murmured.

The stallion rolled his eyes at her and backed up.

Now the cane was spooking him. No doubt its sim-
ilarity to a length of pipe, she thought. But at the
moment, she needed it, so she spoke in low tones
and moved in slow motion as she herded him toward
the open barn door.

Though he bucked once in protest, his rear hooves
never came near her. Had someone else tried this, it
would have been a different story—an injury, possibly worse. The stallion was powerful enough to
kill. And he was crazed, perhaps permanently. He no
longer could differentiate between friend and foe.

Once inside the barn, he had no choices. She had
blockaded the area so that he could only go directly
into his own stall without passing the few mares still
stabled there. She had actually moved half of them
to another barn so as to cause the least amount of
disturbance.

Whatever it took, she thought. Anything, *anything,* to restore him to Finn mac Cumhail, to his former self. If not, all was lost.

Him.

Grantham Acres.

Herself.

Then, again, perhaps it was too late for her...or for any of them.

Setting fresh oats in his feeder, she crooned, "Come, Finn. Come to me and be my lad."

He'd obviously had enough of human company, even hers, for he turned his back on her and shoved a nose in the corner, where he lipped at some invisible treat on the wood.

Jane's mood darkened.

She wasn't making any headway with the stallion, and she was the only human he would even tolerate. That brutal night had, in some strange way, bonded Finn to her. Only she could enter his stall or feed him or groom him, though at times he made that impossible, too. His trust was limited by the fear that lay just below the surface, always ready to explode. At least one trainer whom she'd gotten to work with Finn had taken his life in his hands—Finn had cornered him and threatened him with bared teeth.

Now Finn's life was in her hands alone.

An impossible burden.

Sighing, her shoulders sagging under an invisible weight, Jane turned from the stallion and left the barn.

Not wanting to face her grandmother or her sister, Susan, who should be home from the day's compulsory summer-school session by now, she crossed the yard to the farm office, where she meant to go over the books yet again.

Perhaps she had missed something. Some money she could use to pay the most imminent bills.

Entering the office, whose walls were wainscoted with the same deep mahogany that lined the insides of all three lavishly executed barns, she stopped square in the middle of the Turkish rug that softened her footfall. The leather chair behind her heavy wooden desk was occupied, and while its back was to her, it wasn't empty.

The light cast through the arched windows illuminated a muscular arm and a powerful hand holding the framed photograph from her desk—her with her parents, taken just before Daddy had died.

"Who are you...and what do you think you're doing?"

The man who whirled around in her chair to meet her angry gaze was black-Irish handsome. Dark hair spilled over a high forehead and equally dark eyebrows arched over intense blue eyes. His smile forced a dimple into his right cheek, giving him a roguish air.

"Getting to know all I can about Grantham Acres," came a soft reply. He set down the framed photograph where it belonged. "Curran McKenna, at your service."

"Curran McKenna," she echoed. "The trainer?"

"The same."

Her mind raced. Finn. He was here because of the Irish Thoroughbred, she was certain. But why? How? Had news of the stallion's madness spread all the way to Ireland? Had he come to claim the truth?

"Explain."

"When I received a letter from you," he began, the Gaelic lilt to his voice becoming suddenly more pronounced, "asking for my help—"

"I wrote you no letter!"

"But you are needing my help, now, aren't you?"

Her denial didn't seem to faze him. Suddenly it all came clear to her. "Nani…my grandmother. She's the one who invited you to come here."

"So she told me a while ago."

"Look, Mr. McKenna—"

"Curran."

"I'm sorry for your trouble, but I can't use you." He was an A-list trainer with world-class clients. "I'm sorry you've come on a fool's errand. I'll reimburse you for your plane tickets and any other expenses—"

He waved a hand. "Not necessary."

"—but you'll have to go."

"Why?"

"Because I say so!"

Exasperated, she wished he would just leave. She wasn't about to humiliate herself by explaining that she couldn't afford his services.

That she would have to top off one of her credit cards just to see him home.

That she had lost all hope and dared not believe in another stranger.

"And what of your grandmother?" Curran asked. "Don't her wishes have any merit? She apparently went through some trouble to get me here."

"She was trying to help."

"Aye. As am I."

If only that were possible. "You can't."

"Not if you won't let me try."

"Finn won't let anyone but me come near him. Several highly respected trainers in the area have already tried and failed. To be truthful, I'm lucky that I don't have a lawsuit on my hands over injuries."

"But *I* have not yet tried."

He didn't even pretend to hide his arrogance. Jane crossed her arms over her chest and challenged him with a fierce stare, which he met head-on.

Trainers who had worked with her breeder father before her had vested themselves in trying to help her for the sake not only of his memory but for Grantham Acres itself, a respected breeding farm in the Lexington area for more than a century. All to no avail. All had given up with the same advice to her—to put down the dangerous stallion.

She moved in to the desk so she could get a better look at the man who thought so highly of himself. Up close, he was even more devastatingly handsome than she'd realized, a fact that set her nerves on edge.

"And what, may I ask, is so special about you?"

He grinned. "I do have a reputation."

"Yes," she said dryly, even as her pulse surged at an awareness that she deemed inappropriate. He had a different beautiful woman on his arm at every photo op. She read any paper or magazine possible if it had to do with Thoroughbreds and racing, and so she had seen many such photographs over the past three years. "I am aware of your reputation. But what does that have to do with Finn mac Cumhail?"

"When I was working for Maggie Butler, I was the one who handpicked him at the yearling sale."

"*You* trained Finn?"

"Gentled him, yes."

A ray of hope broke through her dark mood. Finn *knew* Curran McKenna.

So what? an internal voice asked. *Finn only trusts you and not very far at that.*

Realistically, Curran McKenna would still be the enemy, Jane realized. And then she would have put Finn through more agony for nothing. No, her best bet was to keep working with him herself. She was the only one who had a chance of getting through to the stallion.

"I'm sorry, but my mind is made up," she said firmly. "You need to leave at once."

Curran rose and rounded the desk so that he stood inches from her. Though she was taller than average, Jane had to crane her neck to look up at him. He stared into her face as though studying her—for what, she couldn't fathom. She only knew that he made her horribly uncomfortable.

And she wouldn't show her discomfort by stepping back as she wanted.

A test of wills. Why?

And why did the trainer's very presence disturb her anyway? she wondered, knowing the sooner he was off the property, the better for her.

When he finally stepped away and left with only a nod, she felt much like a deflating balloon. Tension poured from her in a rush and she sagged back against the desk for support.

Jane stared at the door for a moment, fully expecting Curran McKenna to step back inside to renew the argument.

That he didn't almost disappointed her.

She got hold of herself and rounded the desk, her intention to get at the farm books. But upon sitting in her chair, she felt the leather was still warm, and the air around it filled with Curran's male scent.

Shaking the sensation was more difficult than it should have been. His presence lingered like a soft caress. Only when she noted her desk calendar did she pierce the veil.

The pages were turned to the wrong date. Someone—Curran McKenna?—had flipped the pages forward two weeks. But what reason would the trainer have had to rifle through her appointments?

The open entry knotted her stomach—the date was that of the Thoroughbred Millions. The very date Finn mac Cumhail might have saved Grantham Acres.

Jane only prayed that she hadn't brought him and the farm itself to ruin.

JANE GRANTHAM WAS an open book.

The new trainer Curran McKenna wasn't.

Hoping one of the mares wouldn't give him away, he slid from the shadows in the barn and made his way to the back exit, where he fled into the open and across the pasture, over the fence and into the woods.

He hadn't expected complications.

Curran McKenna—why the hell was he here?

For the stallion, of course. He'd gentled the chestnut once and no doubt intended on working his magic on the animal a second time.

McKenna's presence gave him pause. It complicated things, and the situation was overly complicated now.

He would just have to be careful.

Act with impunity…but act he would. Whatever it took.

His time was running out.

Chapter Two

"Why doesn't Jane want me to work with Finn?" Curran asked Belle Grantham when he joined her in the drawing room of the main house for a before-dinner drink.

Claiming he had some old cronies to look up, Ned was off to some pub in Lexington for the evening, so it was just Curran and the family.

"I don't profess to know my granddaughter's mind," Belle said, handing him a bourbon.

She busied herself straightening the liquor bottles on an antique cart. This evening, she wore a flowing dress and seemed very much at home in this elegant room.

Fringed pillows lined a curved clay and cream sofa that wrapped around one corner. A chandelier hung from the thirteen-foot ceiling. And a baby grand piano was nestled into a corner alcove, backed by an ebony screen with gold-leaf overlay. Portraits graced one of the clay-colored walls, not of people but of horses.

"I think you know your own blood well enough." Curran took a seat in the chair next to the fireplace, the mantel of carved black marble. "She'll be needing my help with Finn, then. She admitted as much before she told me to leave.''

If not in so many words. He'd sensed Jane Grantham's emotional swing in a very visceral way, and he wasn't about to dismiss any possibilities. Not yet. Not until he got to the bottom of things. And then he would decide.

''She's very proud.''

''And troubled,'' Curran added.

''Yes…well.''

If Belle knew more than she'd indicated earlier, she wasn't forthcoming. Suspecting he had at least some idea of the problem—having seen for himself some major signs of neglect in the farm buildings and knowing the stalls in one of the three barns were all empty—Curran took a sip of his Kentucky bourbon and changed tactics.

''So, you've lived on this glorious estate for how long?''

Brightening, she sat at the edge of the couch, a glass of red wine in hand. ''Since I was a young woman. I was nineteen when I married Lawrence.''

''You were involved in the business.''

''I still am. Actively. If I retired, what in heaven's name would I do with myself?''

Guessing that despite her youthful looks, Belle was in her early seventies, Curran gave her credit for being able to handle such physically demanding work. Probably the very thing that kept her young, he thought.

Taking another sip of his drink, he casually said, ''So if something should happen to Grantham Acres…''

Curran knew that he'd hit a nerve when Belle immediately paled and set down her wine next to several books on horses and farms that lay spread across the glass coffee table.

"Nothing is going to happen to my home," she said, sounding more determined than convinced.

"I'm not meaning to be presumptuous, now," Curran said, "but this place needs some serious upkeep. That requires money, which, begging your pardon, you don't seem to have. And yet the purchase price on Finn mac Cumhail must have been nearly a million dollars."

The stallion had impeccable bloodlines as Curran full well knew. While Finn had been sidelined from winning the Irish Derby due to an injury, he had been a favorite. And then, under another trainer, he'd gone on to win several important European Group I races in the past two years.

"Plus, I've not been hearing rumors of his being retired from the racing circuit," Curran continued, "so it's a bit curious that a breeding farm would be buying him. I suspect that you were counting on entering him in the Thoroughbred Millions Classic."

Horses from Britain and Ireland and the Emirates and even Japan would be flown in for the annual day of high purse, Grade I races that was to be run at Churchill Downs this year. The four-million-dollar Classic would be the crowning event of the day and would put turf horses alongside those that normally ran on a dirt track.

Silent for a moment, Belle blinked and her eyes grew fluid. Her lips trembled as she admitted, "That was the plan. We had to take a second mortgage on Grantham Acres to buy Finn. Jane's father left us in so much debt. I loved my son, but I knew his faults.

I never should have let Frederick take over the finances. He not only loved breeding horses, he loved betting on them, as well." She sighed. "Jane was left with too large a burden for such a young woman. When he died three years ago, she was barely twenty-five."

"And there was no one else to lend a hand?"

"The farm never interested her brother, Andrew, who is too wrapped up in getting his MBA in Chicago to worry about what's going on here. While Jane's sister, Susan, loves the horses, she's only seventeen years old and is still in high school. And their mother, Lydia, remarried last winter and moved to North Carolina. So we're the farm, Jane and I. Three years of hard work barely chipped away at that debt."

"And you thought Finn's winning the Classic would be your solution?"

"He doesn't even need to win. He merely has to come in the money. Then we would retire him to stud. Between the purse and the stud fees and the colts and fillies we could get from a few of our own top mares, we thought we could have the farm back on its feet in no time."

Frederick Grantham wasn't the only gambler in the family, Curran thought. "Then everything rides on whether or not Finn can perform."

Belle nodded. "And you were our last hope to make that happen."

"I'm not sure your granddaughter will be sharing that sentiment."

"Yes, she would if only she weren't so proud. What's troubling her, Curran, is that you're a top trainer and we can't afford to pay you. My hope was

that, since you had a bond with the horse, you
wouldn't want to see him destroyed. I was going to
offer you a larger cut of the purse than normal for
your services.''

Which would reduce the return on their investment.

If Finn got in the money.

If the stallion were even viable to race.

And *if* Jane Grantham would put her pride second
to Finn's welfare.

As if his thoughts summoned her, an uneven tread
and *tap-tap* from the foyer alerted Curran to her arrival.

''Nani, you won't believe what Susan did this
time!''

The moment Jane limped into the room, cane in
hand, she spotted him. Stopping short, she blinked,
her thick, dark lashes flicking over golden-brown
eyes gone round.

Her eyes were her best feature, he thought. While
the rest of her face was attractive, her eyes could
captivate a man across a crowded room. Suddenly
the blood rushed through him, thick and hot like a
volcano flow.

As if she could sense what he was feeling, she
white-knuckled the silver horse's head topping her
cane. A flush crept up from the V neckline of her
short-sleeved sweater, a rich gold that brought out
the highlights in her hair. That her sun-kissed skin
took on a rosy glow—irritation or embarrassment?—
both amused and beguiled Curran.

But if she were captivated in return, she hid it well.
For the first words out of her full mouth, now painted

a tempting soft berry, were "What are you still doing here?"

"Jane!" Belle protested. "Curran is our guest!"

"Yes, of course. Turning him out before feeding him wouldn't be polite."

Her snipe broke the tension, and Curran laughed.

Jane moved closer, and he could see she was trying to control her gait as if nothing was wrong. Still, there was that barely perceptible dip each time her left foot shot forward. And she was practically crushing the horse's head.

Then she was in his space and something bumped at his psyche, startling him as it had in the pasture that morning. Only earlier, he'd put it to Finn.

If only he could touch her to explore the impulse...but how to do so without raising her hackles?

Even without touch, the awareness of connection grew demanding and sharp, but Jane didn't give him time to explore the perception.

"I thought we had an understanding."

"You made a demand that I head for home. I merely chose not to argue with you."

"I am the farm manager," she reminded him. "What goes on here is up to me."

"As well it should be. And I am certain that as the farm manager, you will do what is best for Grantham Acres. And especially for Finn."

He didn't add *rather than for yourself.* But from the way her lovely mouth pursed tight, he was certain that she understood exactly what he meant.

"So...how would you handle him?"

Ignoring the terseness of her question, he played with her. "Trying to pry my secrets out of me?"

"You wouldn't have much time to work with him. The Thoroughbred Millions is coming up fast."

Curran was encouraged that she was challenging him at all. No matter her protest, she was interested.

"No one can get near Finn, yet you have plans to race him?" he asked.

"Too much for you to handle?"

"Are you planning to run him without a jockey on his back?"

Again, she flushed. "If you were to train him, getting one on his back would be up to you. Or maybe it's too much to expect."

The arrival of Susan Grantham temporarily stopped further debate. The teenager swept into the room wearing a pale apricot dress with full skirts. Curran considered the romantic look at odds with her short, spiked brown hair and multiple ear piercings.

"You see what I mean, Nani," Jane said, abruptly turning her full attention to her younger sister. "Now she's taken over my wardrobe."

"Why not? You never wear your dresses anymore," Susan said. "You're too afraid someone will see the scars on your leg."

Even as Jane paled, Belle said, "Susan, that's enough. Where are your manners?"

"My sisters had the same problem." Curran smoothly prevented the teenager from stirring up more hurt in the sister she undoubtedly loved. "Flanna used to drive our older sister Keelin mad by borrowing her clothes without asking permission. More than once, Keelin threatened Flanna's demise. Better yet, she got even with her. One day Flanna came home from school to find that her closet had been stripped of every item, and Keelin claimed innocence for days.''

''Now there's an idea,'' Jane murmured, her lips softening into an engaging smile.

Susan ignored her sister and zeroed in on him. ''Who are you anyway? Are you really from Ireland or is that accent put on? And what on earth are you doing here?''

''Susan!''

Belle took over and made brief introductions before the girl could continue with her rapid-fire interrogation that only served to amuse Curran. He suspected the teenager kept life lively in this household of women.

Then they all moved past eleven-foot-high pocket doors into the dining room, where vermilion wallpaper with touches of gold provided a perfect backdrop for the Sheraton-style dining table and heavily carved Hepplewhite chairs. At the far end, the fireplace mantel was a match to the one in the drawing room. The table itself was set with vermilion and gold place mats, fine china, crystal and silver flatware.

The kind of table his mother might have set for a holiday or special occasion, Curran thought, wondering if the Granthams sat down to such finery every day, or if his being there deemed the dinner special. At least to Belle.

His mother had always done her own cooking, however. The Granthams had Melisande Stams.

''We couldn't do without Melisande,'' Belle said, her voice filled with affection as the woman carried in a tureen of soup. ''She's the chatelaine of Grantham Acres now that Lydia has gone on to her new life.''

"Someone's gotta be looking after this house when you're out with them horses of yours.''

Melisande's melodic tones reminded Curran of the islands, Caribbean rather than British. And her dress was a cut and print of the exotic variety, the purple and green more brilliant for the contrast with her dark skin. A half-dozen bracelets jangled against the hand that ladled the soup from the tureen.

"Seafood chowder again?'' Susan complained.

"You have a problem with my food, child, you don't have to eat it,'' Melisande said. "You can go hungry.''

Making Curran realize that her standing in the household was more than that of paid help.

"She's so bossy,'' Susan told him. "I don't know why Udell puts up with it.''

"Because her husband loves her as we all do,'' Belle said, explaining, "Udell Stams is the head groom, Curran. You'll be meeting him tomorrow morning.''

"Oh, but he won't have time,'' Jane announced. "He'll need to get to the airport early to make a connection for Shannon in New York or Boston.''

Belle frowned. "Can we leave this discussion until later?''

"There's nothing to discuss!''

As he had in the farm office, Curran kept his own counsel. For the moment.

She switched subjects. "Phyllis Singleton-Volmer called today,'' Belle told Jane. "You forgot to confirm that you'll attend her pre-Millions party tomorrow night.''

"I wasn't planning on attending."

"Grantham Acres needs to be represented not just by me but by the farm manager. You are, after all, still hoping to race Finn in the Classic. Mukhtar Saladin and Holt Easterling will certainly be there."

Curran knew the Saudi owner and his British trainer well. Their Classic Cup entry, Stonehenge, was one of the favorites. He'd also won the Irish Derby the year Curran had to withdraw Finn. But he remembered reading that Finn had beat Stonehenge in the Prix Noailles at Longchamp in early April. Now both horses would be making their dirt debut together—*if* Finn raced.

The challenge to him personally was becoming interesting.

"Besides," Belle went on, "local trainers didn't turn their backs on you when you arrived home from New York with a crazed horse."

"No one actually was able to help Finn."

"That doesn't negate the fact that they tried, Jane." Belle's tone brooked no argument when she added, "And you will not make me look foolish by going back on my word. You will attend the party. For me, if not for yourself."

Curran could tell that Jane wasn't happy about the order, but she didn't argue. Belle glanced his way and he gave her a reassuring look to convey that he wouldn't let her granddaughter dissuade him from his purpose, either.

Unless he was satisfied that he *couldn't* help Finn, he wasn't going anywhere.

TENSE THROUGHOUT DINNER, Jane picked at her food. That's all the appetite she had with Curran

McKenna at her elbow. A table that sat twelve and he was practically on top of her. And she didn't even want to be in the same room with him.

Thankfully, Melisande removed their plates with no more than a *tch-tch* at seeing the leftovers on hers. The housekeeper was opting for subtle in front of company.

Company...

Not so thankfully, she still had to deal with the Irish horse trainer.

He'd stared at her throughout the meal. He was staring at her now. Why? And why was she so susceptible to his regard? Certain he was trying to hit a nerve, she had to admit he was succeeding.

Springing up from the table without warning, Susan announced, "I'm out of here."

"What about your homework?"

"Done!"

"Be home by ten," Jane told her, knowing that, without boundaries, her sister tended to run wild.

Susan flashed her an irritated look but didn't argue. No doubt she feared being grounded again. Instead, she turned her back on Jane, kissed their grandmother's cheek and rushed out of the house.

Jane waited until coffee was served before asking, "So when *will* you be leaving for Ireland, Curran?"

"That's up to you."

"You could have fooled me."

Expecting another sharp reproach, she glanced at her grandmother, who seemed intent on stirring the cream in her coffee to death.

"I have a proposition, if you would care to be hearing it," Curran said.

Suspicious of his placating tone, not to mention

the way he seemed to be looking through her, she asked, "What kind of proposition?"

"The usual kind, where we each get what we want or need. I work with Finn on a contingency basis."

"What contingency?"

"When he wins the Thoroughbred Millions Classic—"

"You can't guarantee that," she cut in.

"When he wins," Curran repeated, "I get one-third of his share of the purse."

"That's outrageous!"

"It's called a gamble," Belle said, suddenly rising from the table. "I'll let the two of you work out the details on your own."

Jane gaped as the older woman headed for the doorway. Curran was *her* idea. How could her grandmother abandon her like this?

"Oh, I nearly forgot." She stopped and turned back to them. "About Phyllis's party—I told her that Curran would be escorting us."

Stunned, Jane didn't know what to say. Arguing with her grandmother was a waste of breath. Besides, she'd already left the room.

Turning her focus back on the Irishman, she noted that he was staring at her again, as if he was trying to get inside her. Her breath caught in her throat and her pulse surged. That did it! She struggled to her feet.

"I could use some air."

Fresh air would be just the thing to clear her head and give her some perspective. Not to mention some distance from the man who leaned in a tad too close, reviving memories she'd rather not revisit. She grabbed her cane and used it to get her out of the dining room.

Curran followed her through the foyer and out the front door to the portico. There, she wedged a shoulder against one of the columns and stared through the dusk over the land she'd loved all her life.

Losing Grantham Acres was unthinkable.

"If Finn doesn't make money," Curran began again, "it costs you nil. I go back to Ireland with nothing to show for my trouble. But if he does win, I get a bonus."

"A very large bonus."

"As it stands, you don't have a chance in hell of so much as getting Finn to the gate."

Jane knew he was right. She turned to face him in the waning light. With deepening shadows hiding his eyes, he appeared mysterious. And frightening.

"Why?" she asked softly, now trying to read him. Turnabout was only fair. What did he really want out of this partnership? "Why would you work for weeks when chances of Finn's winning and your making money are slim to none?"

"I believe in myself. More than that, I believe in Finn mac Cumhail. He should have won the Irish Derby for me, but he was sidelined due to an injury. And then he was taken out of my hands and given to another trainer. I would like another try at being there with him for a major victory."

So there it was, she thought cynically: pride.

The Irish horse trainer's pride bade him try again with the one that got away. Well, his seemingly generous offer now made more sense, anyway. And it made her feel a bit better about seriously considering it.

"And what if he doesn't win?" she asked, wanting to know all the particulars. "What if he merely places or shows? Same deal?"

"Then you can keep his share of the purse."

That stopped her again. Curran McKenna certainly had some ego. "You're that sure you can pull it off?"

"No one can be certain about the outcome of a horse race. There are too many factors to tally in. What I am certain of is that Finn is too special to destroy."

Her temper flared. "I don't care what anyone says! I would never destroy him!"

Considering what they'd been through together, it would be like destroying a part of herself.

"Perhaps not, but fate can be cruel. That decision could be taken out of your hands."

How well she knew that. If they lost Grantham Acres and Finn with it, someone else would have the say. She'd already heard what other trainers recommended. And it would be all her fault.

Finn was their only chance. His own only chance. But he needed help.

He needed Curran McKenna.

And as much as she hated admitting it, that meant she did, as well.

"Tomorrow morning at eight," she said abruptly. "Meet me at the paddock and we'll see how it goes."

No promises. Merely a tryout, she told herself. But she couldn't help hoping anyway.

"One morning? You have to be realistic, Jane. You can't expect a miracle."

But a miracle was exactly what she needed.

Jane held out her hand to seal the deal.

Curran locked gazes as he reached out, seemingly in slow motion. As his flesh slipped over hers, she started. The contact was potent. A surge of something strange and frightening made her want to pull her hand free. To step out of his seductive aura. To protect herself.

But he held fast and her impulse to fight him waned.

His gentle touch was as intimate as any embrace.

Warmth flowed through her, and for a moment, her world went off kilter. Her breath grew shallow, and the thud of her heart filled her ears.

Fool! Jane silently chastised herself, realizing her body was betraying her, growing taut with an unnamed yearning. She was attracted to the man and there didn't seem to be anything she could do about it.

JANE'S RAPID PULSE shot from her wrist through Curran's fingertips. Again he was beset by the sensation that had startled him that morning—the one he normally got only with horses.

So, it hadn't come from Finn, after all.

He concentrated and his own pulse changed tempo in unison with hers.

Fear…longing…anger…

A spray of black across a silvered night. Blood? Hers or Finn's?

Trying to explore deeper, he was stopped cold… Curran let go of her hand and resisted the impulse to slide his arms around her and just hold her.

Jane Grantham had built walls of protection around her as sturdy as her iron will. He could knock at those walls all he wanted, but until she was ready—or off guard, as she had been when he'd watched her with the stallion—she wouldn't be welcoming him in.

"Tomorrow morning, then," he said, backing off, his pulse steadying.

"At eight."

Curran left her standing there, arms curled around her middle, as if she was determined to shield her inner self from him.

Surely she couldn't know…

The "gift" that he'd inherited from his grandmother Moira wasn't something he advertised.

He hurried toward the guest house, his stride reflecting his satisfaction in having masked his true intentions when he'd negotiated with Jane about the purse. He'd let her save face. Better that she feel as though she was being taken than feel as if she was taking charity from a stranger. He doubted that her pride would have allowed that.

The money wasn't the important thing here. Finn was. And Jane Grantham herself.

She and the stallion seemed bound by the mysterious "accident" that she kept secret. A secret that he needed to know—*would* know—if he was to help them.

His gift had never meant so much as it did now. And somehow, it had mutated to include Jane Grantham. Or would include her if he found a way in.

Could that be what Moira McKenna had meant in her deathbed letter to him?

Curran thought about the possibility as he approached the two-story guest house that had probably been meant to serve as the farm manager's quarters, assuming the manager hadn't also been the owner. Three bedrooms, two baths, eat-in country kitchen with a woodstove, large living room and dining room with French doors opening onto a covered porch.

Comfortable digs that pleased him, especially since the porch overlooked the three stables and paddocks.

Not that he would be there long. Two weeks at best.

Upon entering the house, he went straight upstairs to the main bedroom and his shoulder bag, yet unpacked. He pulled out his trainer's journal, whose pages were filled with notes on horses he'd worked with and thoughts on training techniques.

In a plastic sleeve attached to the back cover, the journal housed the letter.

Sitting down on the edge of the bed, he unfolded the worn missive that he'd read hundreds of times since his Grandmother Moira's death.

To my darling Curran,

I leave you my love and more. Within thirty-three days of your thirty-third birthday—enough time to know what you are about—you will have in your grasp a legacy of which your dreams are made. Dreams are not always tangible things, but more often are born in the heart. Act selflessly in another's behalf, and my legacy will be yours.

Your loving grandmother,
Moira McKenna

P.S. Use any other inheritance from me wisely and only for good, lest you destroy yourself or those you love.

Curran knew his grandmother had left the same message for each of her nine grandchildren, but every time he read the letter she'd written to him, he could hear her beloved voice lilt through his mind. And he could imagine she was speaking to him alone.

Act selflessly in another's behalf...

Selfless had been his grandmother's life code. She had helped heal any injured creature that came her way, whether animal or human.

In reading the letter, he'd always believed she'd meant the horses—he'd gotten his love for Irish Thoroughbreds and his understanding of them from Moira herself. From the time he was a child, he'd had a special bond with them through his gift. For a while, he'd shared that bond until playmates deemed him crackers, even as disbelieving, rude adults had called Moira a crazy old hag.

And so he had learned to keep the equine whisperings to himself.

The gift had served him well. Mostly.

And now it was time to pay back. To use Moira's inheritance selflessly as she had deemed proper.

Moira had *known* things, Curran remembered.

Could she have foreseen his second chance to make Finn into a winner? A Classic Cup triumph would be a dream come true, but what was *the* dream she meant?

As for the other possibility—her so-called legacy of love and danger—Curran couldn't help but be skeptical considering the shambles of his one venture in a love relationship.

And yet his sister Keelin and cousins, Skelly, Kathleen and Donovan all swore by the prediction.

Each of them had overcome great dangers to find the loves of their lives.

A nice fairy tale.

But it was too late for him, for today happened to be the thirty-third day after his thirty-third birthday, and the only woman in his life or thoughts was a slightly crazed Jane Grantham.

His time for that part of the legacy had run out.

Chapter Three

When Jane arrived at the barn at eight sharp the next morning, she was disconcerted to find Curran in the middle of the paddock. Disconcerted because he'd brought in a chair and was sitting there and reading the local newspaper rather than making preparations to start working with Finn.

"What in the world are you doing?"

He lowered the paper and raised a dark eyebrow. "I thought it was fairly obvious. Catching up on world events."

Chagrined at his careless attitude toward his odd behavior, she protested, "But you're in the middle of the paddock!"

"Sitting outside the paddock won't get me too close to Finn, now, will it?"

"Why are you sitting at all?"

"Trying to be unobtrusive."

Chagrin advanced straight to irritation. "Well, it isn't working!"

"All right. Make that nonthreatening."

To whom? she wondered. To Finn? Or to her?

Leaning her arms against the fencing, she studied Curran's wickedly handsome features—piercing blue

eyes, engaging mouth drawn into what seemed to be
a knowing smile, dimpling cheek—and tried to de-
bunk the effect they had on her. But the longer she
stared, the stronger her reaction to him. He didn't
even seem to notice the tension. His long legs were
stretched out and crossed at the ankles as if he didn't
have a care in the world. He seemed to have the
corner on relaxed.

Especially when he asked, "Well? Aren't you going to get Finn?"

The casual order was enough to raise her hackles.
"And do what with him?"

"Bring him into the paddock, of course. You're
less of a threat approaching him than I am."

Nothing like stating the obvious. "And you're going to do what?"

He indicated the newspaper. "Read."

Her spirits fell. What a loony Irishman. If he
thought this was a valid method of working with a
half-crazed Thoroughbred, he might as well pack it
in now.

But Finn would be the proof of the thing, so she
went inside the barn and fetched him as ordered. Ba-
sically that meant holding open his stall door and
standing back, while the mares looked on from the
other side of the barn and whickered softly for attention.

"Sorry, girls, it'll be your turn soon," she promised.

Jane set her cane to the side so as not to spook
Finn.

"Come on. Time to stretch your legs. And make
mincemeat of yet another trainer," she muttered.

Not that she wanted him to do any such thing.

Hope had actually crept into her while she'd slept, and she had risen feeling more positive than she had in months.

Now she didn't know what to think.

Eyeing her suspiciously as he did every morning, Finn exited the stall and was out of the barn in a flash. But when he saw the man whose back was to him, he stopped short and whinnied. Then he wheeled around as if to get back inside, but Jane was in the process of closing the barn door. More calmly than she was feeling, she limped to the fence, thinking to climb up and watch the show. And then she remembered that pleasure was no longer allowed her.

Instead, she slipped out the gate and stepped up on the bottom board so she could lean on the fence and watch.

The powerful stallion was vibrating with tension. He pranced, then ran full steam around the perimeter of the paddock several times. Suddenly, he stopped short and faced Curran, who continued to blithely read his newspaper as if he were in the breakfast room having his morning coffee.

The stallion pawed the ground and lowered his head, reminding Jane of a bull ready to charge. A knot tightened her stomach as his neck bowed into an arrow, his head the deadly tip. He *would* charge— she'd seen him do it to other trainers. If Curran had any sense of the danger he was in, he was so nonchalant that she couldn't tell. He continued to read and ignore Finn mac Cumhail as if he weren't there.

Then with a squeal, the stallion was off and Jane prayed that neither horse nor human got hurt.

A red ball of rage, bulging neck extended, mouth open, teeth bared, Finn flew across the paddock.

Catching every nuance, Jane gripped the fence board hard. Then, just as the stallion was within yards of his goal, Curran calmly ruffled the newspaper and looked up.

Finn swerved and barely brushed Curran, who murmured, "Finn, my lad, you need to calm yourself. You've worked yourself into a grand lather," so softly that Jane barely caught his words.

But she swore Curran's mesmerizing voice did the trick. Not only did his gentle words flow down to her toes, but she could see Finn's fury simmer down.

The horse circled once and made another approach, but this time he missed Curran altogether.

"There's a lad. You'll be wanting to pace yourself, then," Curran singsonged in a persuasive tone that set Jane's spine tingling, "or you'll spend yourself out. We have a long day ahead of us."

Finn wasn't so easily convinced. As he swept around the arena yet again, mane and tail flashing in the full sun, she followed until a middle-aged man with reddish-brown hair watching from the other side of the paddock caught her attention. Her gaze hesitated on him. He must be Ned Flaherty, Curran's assistant whom she hadn't yet met. Though why he'd brought an assistant for one horse that no one but she could touch, Jane didn't know. For the Thoroughbred Millions, if they made it that far, she guessed.

Something kept her staring at Ned for a moment—he seemed so familiar. From another Kentucky farm? From one of the tracks? But he'd just come from Ireland with Curran.

Unable to place Ned, Jane tucked the question

away as Finn advanced on Curran a third time, and she refocused her attention where it belonged.

"Surely you're tiring of this game, now," Curran said, deliberately crossing one leg over the other.

Finn wheeled and gave him a wide berth and slowed to a walk, stopping near Jane. He stood there, closer to her than normal, as if he trusted in her protection. He was a true herd animal. As frightened as he was of most humans, he still had the instincts to protect himself by becoming one of a group.

A group of two, she thought with irony. And the moment that she would reach out to make a true connection, he would be off again. So she held herself back. Held her breath to see what Curran would do next.

What Curran did next was sing.

He set down the newspaper at his feet and began singing the words to "Oh, Danny Boy," substituting "Finny" for "Danny."

At first Jane was aghast, but her dismay was soon replaced by amusement. And Finn was tuning in to the song—his ears rotated like twin antennae as he listened to the silky tenor. After a few minutes of Curran's crooning, the stallion snorted and nodded his big head as if in approval. And the muscles beneath his red hide seemed to soften.

Jane began to relax, as well.

Maybe Curran McKenna knew what he was doing, after all.

When he'd finished, Curran picked up his newspaper again. "Perhaps you could let Finn back into the barn, then."

Despite the fact that he'd surrendered to the serenade, the stallion was happy to comply.

Jane was just closing his stall gate when her head groom entered the barn through the far exit. He was a narrow man and his dark head was bald. He was as quiet and unassuming as his wife was bossy and colorful. She waved him over.

"Udell, I have someone I want you to meet."

He ambled down the aisle toward her. "The Irishman."

"Melisande told you about him?"

"She said Mrs. Grantham has great faith in him. I got a look at his technique on the way over here. Curious," was all he said about it.

Jane couldn't argue with that. And Udell said nothing further. She appreciated that he took his time when analyzing a situation. He didn't make rash judgments about horses or people.

When they exited the barn, Curran was talking to his assistant. The closer she got to Ned, the more certain she was that she'd seen him somewhere. The bushy reddish-brown eyebrows were especially familiar.

"I'm not feeling right about this, Curran." Ned's arms were crossed over his burly chest and he was frowning. "I'm not used to standing around and whistling in the wind."

"I have nothing for you here at the moment," Curran said. "I need to establish myself with Finn before introducing you to him."

"I could see that."

"But what you could do is drive over to Louisville, get the feel for Churchill Downs."

Ned seemed to roll the idea around, then asked, "You're that sure you can have Finn ready for the Classic?"

"I'm feeling more confident now, yes, though our success will also depend on finding the right jockey. You could ask around—"

Jane joined the conversation. "The top jockeys are already spoken for."

"I didn't say *top,* I said *right.* We're going to need someone who can do nothing but work with Finn once I get him to accept a rider."

Which meant even more money. Jane sighed. This was to be an all-or-nothing proposition, so she might as well stop worrying about every dollar.

"I'll be on my way, then," Ned said, bowing out.

Curran waved him off.

Jane was worried about the jockey situation. "Finn has to be able to take more than one rider."

Any jockey that would be free to work with him to ready him for the race probably wouldn't be the level of jockey needed to win it.

"Of course. Just not in time for the Classic. The safer he feels, the better."

A statement that revved up her nerves again. Surely he wasn't serious. She shook away the negativity. One thing at a time. First, Curran would have to be able to touch Finn, to halter, bridle and saddle him. And Finn was as far as he could be from being ready for all that.

Udell finally stepped forward and let his presence be known. "Jimiyu could do it. He never met a horse that didn't like him."

"Curran, this is Udell Stams, my head groom. Jimi is his son. He's also an apprentice jockey." One who might solve the immediate problem, she thought. "He's always been good with horses from the time he could walk, actually."

"Then it's something to consider. What about his race schedule from now until the Classic in two weeks?"

"He would do anything for the Granthams," Udell said. "He'll make himself available whenever you need him."

"Good."

"Thank you, Udell."

"Gotta get to work now."

The groom backed off, leaving Curran and Jane alone together.

"What now?" she asked.

"We take a break and start again at nine. And then on the hour, every hour, until we make some progress."

"Sounds exhausting."

"That's the point. To exhaust all Finn's energy so he can concentrate on me."

"He *was* concentrating on you."

"But in a negative way. I'm wanting to spark his curiosity."

"'Oh, Finny Boy' did that," she said dryly.

"A technique I developed myself."

His grin got to her. Made her feel breathless and eager for something she didn't want to recognize. Uncomfortable with yet another inappropriate physical response to the Irishman, she whipped away from him and headed for the house.

Over her shoulder, she called, "I'll see you at nine."

At nine, Curran sat in the chair minus the newspaper. He did have a boom box playing traditional Irish music, however. Finn kicked up his heels, but the sheer animosity was gone.

At ten, so was the chair. Curran stood in one spot. Finn eyed him suspiciously and made one attempt to rush him. Speaking to the stallion in a low tone, Curran refused to move. He stood square to Finn and faced him down.

At eleven, Finn stopped coming to Jane for protection, and Curran began moving around the paddock, seemingly paying the stallion no mind.

Finn didn't buy into that until three. A few minutes of watching Curran and he finally began following him.

And Jane could hardly believe her own eyes.

Curran hadn't once tried approaching or touching the stallion. He'd merely used body language and the mellifluous tones of his voice to seduce Finn.

"That's enough for the day, wouldn't you say?" he asked after she'd gotten Finn back into his stall once again.

"Yes," she said. "Truly. I'm in awe."

"Then I have the job?"

Remembering that she'd told him she'd try him out with Finn and then decide, Jane nodded. "One-third of the purse when he wins the Classic."

Curran held out his hand to shake on it, but she backed off, unwilling to get too close. If she wasn't careful, he might try gentling *her*.

CAMOUFLAGED HIGH in the branches of a tree, he lowered the binoculars and traded them for a cell phone. The number was already on his speed dial. Two rings and the connection was made.

"Yes?" came the impatient voice.

"We have a situation here."

"How bad is it?"

"Bad enough. No halter yet. He didn't even try it. But the horse is accepting him. It's only a matter of time. Days. Maybe less."

Curran McKenna was known to have some magic about him when it came to the tough rides. Something to do with some special animal empathy he'd inherited from his grandmother. At least that was the rumor whispered around the tracks. McKenna had never openly admitted to anything other than hard work making his success.

"You know what you have to do!" came the sharp reply. "No more delays."

"You can't rush this. There are too many people around during the day!" he protested, trying to stall. "And at night, the buildings are set up with alarms. I saw the system when I was in the barn yesterday." Though he might have a way around that, he couldn't be sure.

He listened to crackling, typical of a cell-phone connection, long enough to make him sweat.

Finally, his contact said, "Then you'll need to be extra careful so that you don't get caught. But—and I don't say this lightly—you won't fail me if you want to remain free and in a state of good health."

His mood growing darker, he broke the connection.

Threats, he hated them nearly as much as he hated himself for getting into this mess.

CURRAN HADN'T BROUGHT a tux. He refused to wear what to him was a symbol of a dark time in his life— two years of dancing to the tune of a woman to whom appearances had been everything. And to whom he had been, in the end, nothing.

Now he didn't have to dance to anyone's tune but his own.

So, while the pale gray silk-blend suit and charcoal-gray silk T-shirt would be considered inappropriate by most at the society party given by the Singleton-Volmer woman, he would be comfortable in his own skin.

And when he entered the foyer of the main house, he had to give Jane credit that she didn't so much as blink at his unconventional attire.

"My grandmother forgot something," she said distractedly. "She'll be ready to leave in a moment."

She seemed preoccupied. An attack of nerves at appearing at a society gathering because of a minor disability? Curran wondered.

Jane Grantham didn't have to worry, she was a natural Kentucky Thoroughbred. Despite the flat sandals and cane, both concessions to the injury that still plagued her, she was a study in grace and elegance: upswept hairdo that neatly framed her face; simple dress that flowed along her perfect curves like molten gold; understated makeup that accentuated her broad mouth and high cheekbones.

But her wide-set amber eyes were clouded tonight, and Curran couldn't help but wonder what memories caused such pain. As he stared into them, he thought about holding her in his arms and sweeping her slowly around a dance floor. About feeling the beat of her heart against his. About losing himself in the light fragrance that made him want to get closer now.

He could make love to her there, without ever taking her to bed...

Suddenly aware of his scrutiny, she snapped,

"What? If you have something to say, then out with it!"

Making Curran think he was going to have one hell of an evening, one way or another.

As he had done with Finn earlier, he squared himself with Jane and looked her straight in the eye. "I was thinking that you looked grand and elegant and would undoubtedly put the hostess to shame."

She had the grace to blush at his soft words. And like Finn, she backed off, her gaze going to something over his shoulder. She headed straight past him, only to stop at a spindly-legged table tucked into the corner of the foyer, where she sorted through the day's mail as if she hadn't seen it earlier when he knew she had.

Her back stayed firmly turned to him, again reminding him of Finn's maneuvers.

Part of Curran was amused, part rueful that she should be so combative and unsure of herself. Certain that she hadn't always been that way, even as Finn hadn't, he wondered what had happened to her.

Why was she so guarded that she attacked before even knowing what was on his mind?

There was another way, he thought, remembering the flood of emotion that he'd sensed when he'd watched her the day before. But though he concentrated, he couldn't get a read, not without touching her.

If only he could touch her, he might be able to breach the barrier she'd set between them. But forcing any contact now would only raise the level of antagonism between them.

Luckily, he was a patient man.

Gentling Jane would be more of a challenge than the stallion, Curran mused.

Not that he'd ever used the techniques on a woman before. Nor had he known he could. Until now, his empathic abilities had been reserved for animals, primarily Thoroughbreds. Jane Grantham was an exception and he had to admit the temptation to explore that factor was too strong to resist.

"Here I am at last," Belle said as she entered the room, wearing a bronze-colored gown that barely swept the floor behind her. "Somehow I always manage to displace at least one thing a day, and of course at the most inconvenient time."

"Ah, but the wait was worth it," Curran said. He took Belle's ringed hand and held it out so that he could admire her openly. "The Grantham women are marvels. I certainly will be the luckiest escort at the party with the two of you as my companions."

Jane gave him a sour look, but Curran didn't miss the glow of color along her neckline.

On the ride to Rolling Meadows Farm, he concentrated his attention on Belle, who gave him a quick update on the evening's festivities. Phyllis Singleton-Volmer was one of the most noted hostesses in the Lexington area, and her parties were always social highlights of the racing season.

"It will be outdoors, of course," Belle said. "All those people wouldn't fit in her house."

"Dining and dancing under the stars sounds very romantic, don't you think?" he asked Jane, looking up into the rearview mirror to see her reaction.

"Actually, it sounds exhausting. We've had a long day and it will be another early morning. I'll be making my excuses as early as graciously possible."

"You didn't used to be so difficult, Jane," Belle complained.

"That was another lifetime, Nani, and I was another person."

"Well, I wish you would hurry and reacquaint yourself with the lost Jane again."

Jane didn't answer, merely stared out the side window into the dusk.

A moment later, Belle instructed Curran to slow down and turn up a long gravel driveway. On a rise, the house was lit, and spread around it, large tents played host to hundreds of people. Insurance against the elements, he thought, though the evening's weather was perfect.

Phyllis Singleton-Volmer was holding court at the garden entrance, and Curran immediately recognized the Saudi Thoroughbred owner at her side.

"Why, Belle, you look lovely tonight," Phyllis gushed. "Let me introduce you to my special friend, Mukhtar Saladin." Her glance at him was just short of adoring. "Mukhtar owns Stonehenge. I'm sure you've heard of him—the favorite to win the Thoroughbred Millions Classic."

"That's to be seen," Belle said, even as she acknowledged Phyllis's companion with a gracious smile.

They were some couple, Curran thought, sizing them up—she an elegant brunette in her mid- to upper-fifties, very thin, very chic in a strapless red sheath; he, possibly twenty years her senior, a dark and brooding tuxedoed guardian, his face wreathed in a silver-streaked beard and mustache.

Phyllis refocused her attention, her emerald-green

eyes sizing him up. "So this is the famous Curran McKenna. I'm so thrilled to meet you at last."

"Thrilled?" Curran took her proffered hand. Not that she actually grasped him, merely touched her flesh to his. "I'm flattered. But of course this is actually my first trip to the Americas."

"But I travel quite extensively to England and Ireland. Mukhtar insists that I be there for good luck when one of his top Thoroughbreds races."

"He has exquisite taste both in horseflesh and in women," Curran said, noticing that Saladin kept a possessive hand on Phyllis's diamond-bejeweled arm.

"Phyllis is the one who picked out Stonehenge." Saladin raised her hand to his lips. "She insisted I buy him. When it comes to horseflesh, she's the most knowledgeable woman of my acquaintance."

"You make a fine pair, then."

"I certainly think so." Phyllis's voice went husky. "I wouldn't mind being a permanent part of Mukhtar's stable."

They all laughed.

Then a big blond man came up behind Saladin and whispered something in the owner's ear. Holt Easterling was Saladin's British trainer, one whom Curran knew well enough to dislike—a serious difference in training methods. A man with a feral streak that he normally hid well, Easterling wasn't above using force on his horses to get them to do what he wanted.

Curran had called him on it once, so Easterling wasn't fond of him, either. They exchanged dark looks as the Brit pulled Saladin away from the others to confer in private.

"Ah, Jane," Phyllis gushed, "you remind me so

very much of your mother. We went to school together, you know. How is our dear Lydia?''

Curran swore he detected a change in inflection at the last, but her features didn't reflect any ambivalence.

"Mother is deliriously happy in her new marriage.''

"Happy, away from Grantham Acres?''

She sounded shocked, Curran thought, as if moving away from the horse farm was unthinkable.

"The farm was never her life,'' Jane said. "Daddy was. So without him around… But in a way that was better for us both, since I've never thought about doing anything other than working the farm.''

"I see.'' Phyllis's gaze wandered down to the cane. "Then it's a shame that you'll never be able to live up to your full potential.''

Curran felt Jane stiffen at the unexpectedly insensitive observation. But before he could come to her defense, Saladin interrupted.

"You must excuse me, my little raven,'' he said, placing possessive hands on Phyllis's arms. "But I must attend to some pressing business.''

"You won't be long?''

"Would I leave you alone and vulnerable to some predator any longer than absolutely necessary?'' he murmured.

What could be important enough for him to leave his lover's soiree other than a problem with a horse? Curran wondered. Had something happened to Stonehenge? Had Easterling done something to the prized Thoroughbred? Surely not or Mukhtar Saladin would have his head.

Curran glanced at Jane. Outwardly, she seemed to

have recovered from Phyllis's thoughtless remark.
But he was close enough to feel her internal struggle,
her need to keep up a polished veneer, when she
wanted to do nothing more than wheel away from
measuring eyes, even as Finn would.

What bound the two so closely together? he wondered yet again.

Other people had arrived, so Belle led them away
from their hostess along the garden pathway to the
tented festivities and a lively Latin rhythm. Jane went
next and seemed to be walking more easily than she
had that morning, Curran noticed as he brought up
the rear.

Scattered among the crowd before them were a
handful of owners, trainers and jockeys he knew, or
knew of. But oddly enough, he had no interest in
seeking their company. He was content to be with
Jane.

Transference? His long-standing bond with Finn
transferred to her?

Inexplicable, Curran decided.

They came to a stop in an open area. The bar and
buffet lay straight ahead. Tables sat to one side, the
dance floor and live orchestra opposite.

"Why, there's Mitzi Driver," Belle suddenly said,
waving toward the sea of tables. "I haven't seen her
for ages. She's been spending most of her time in
California. You two can get along without me for a
few minutes, can't you?"

Jane started, "We can go with—"

But Curran cut her off. "I'm sure we'll be finding
a way to entertain ourselves."

As Belle picked her way through the crowd, Jane
echoed, "Entertain ourselves?"

"On the dance floor." The rhythm had changed, slower, now, a sultry tango, and was too inviting to resist.

"That may do for *you*."

He took her hand and backed toward the sound of music. "And for you, as well, if you're willing to cling to me."

Though she didn't fight him, she protested. "I cling to no man any longer."

"So I've noticed. I shall be hanging on to you, then."

Before she could protest, he took the cane from her hand and set it to one side, curled an arm around her waist and swept her onto the dance floor.

Chapter Four

Strong emotions washed through Curran. *Hers.*

Jane was panicking—despite herself, when he swung her into his arms, she grabbed on to his hand and fisted the back of his jacket.

But gradually, she relaxed against him as he moved her smoothly, expertly, without so much as a wrong step. She lost herself in the exotic music as it swept them to another place and time.

One with no constraints. No barriers. No disabilities. Just two people savoring the now.

Curran felt her soft, full breasts press into his chest. And her hips undulating to the music brushed his seductively. He breathed in her scent. Wildflowers.

His imagination took him from the dance floor to a Connemara meadow carpeted with wildflowers, where they would compose a horizontal tango of their very own.

He could imagine her sensual expression as she opened her arms to welcome him into her perfect, nude body. He could feel the cadence of her heartbeat change as they were joined, two unto one. He could hear the sounds issuing from deep in her throat as he completed her again and again.

Somehow, he knew making love to her was destined. Then Jane took a wrong step. Curran caught her, held her tighter against him. So tight that he could feel the increasingly rapid beat of her heart.

"Don't fret now, Sheena. You're safe in my arms," he murmured in her ear.

"Sheena?" she gasped, blinking hard, obviously working her way back out of the spell.

"The Irish familiar for Jane."

She pulled her hand from his and pushed against his chest. "I gave you no call to be familiar with me!"

"Ah, but you have, sweet Sheena. Your lips say one thing, but your eyes another."

He looked deep into their amber depths and without warning was whirled into the fearsome darkness of her mind.

Fear...hatred...horror...

A silhouette against the moon-silvered night...a man, his arms raised in threat...a scream, not human...

Agony flashed through his left knee, and his left leg almost gave way. He held on, tried to ride out the pain, but the overwhelming sensation stole away his breath. His head spun and he tried to refocus even as liquid black splashed across the silver backdrop of his inner vision.

Blood?

His heart palpitated.

He found his breath.

And suddenly he was back in the present and the amber eyes were shut against him.

He knew, she thought. Somehow, he knew.

What was Curran doing to her?

What power did he have, for even with her eyes shut, she felt him, larger than life, as if he were a presence deep inside her...

Blinking her eyes open again, she stared at his serious visage hard, but the thing that had happened between them—*unless she had imagined it*—was gone. Confusion made her careless, and the next she knew, she stepped wrong and her knee gave way and she plowed straight into his broad chest. The threat of falling panicked her and made her grasp onto his jacket front.

Before she could guess what he was about, Curran quickly rolled her to one side and bowed her back across his arm as if all along he'd meant to dip her. Then before she could wonder what came next, she was righted and moving to the music as if nothing had ever happened.

And maybe it hadn't.

Maybe she had imagined it.

Maybe she was so man-starved, so sex-starved, that she'd created an impossible bond with the first attractive male who had gotten close enough.

"Good save," she murmured, horrified as always by the idea of humiliating herself in public, grateful that Curran had turned her clumsiness into something that had appeared planned and graceful. "Thank you, Curran."

"My pleasure."

Pleasure was all she felt now that the darkness had receded. He was holding her too close. Too tightly. His movements on the dance floor were thankfully uncomplicated, and yet far too intimate for her peace of mind.

His chest brushing against her breasts raised the tender flesh of her nipples. His hand on her hip made other, more secret places long for his touch. His thigh inserting itself between hers as he took her through a series of easy turns made warmth flow from her center.

Did he know? Could he read her? Did he feel a responding attraction?

Her head was mired in an unexpected haze of sexual excitement, yet at the same time she realized that she was dancing.

Really dancing!

A small triumph, Jane knew, but one she would savor every time she recalled these few moments in Curran's arms. She hadn't known she could do this again without making a fool of herself. Curran had to take all the credit, of course. He made maneuvers that seemed impossible to her, impossibly easy.

Suddenly, the music climaxed and he stopped, chest to breast with her, thigh to thigh.

And the glint from his eyes told her that he felt it, too. An unbearably strong attraction.

Jane blinked and forced herself to breathe.

Gradually…slowly…feeling as if it took a hundred lifetimes…Curran inched back, away from her.

Jane gasped and tried to get hold of herself. To still her awakened body. To quiet her tumultuous thoughts. But flushed and breathless, she couldn't seem to manage it.

Hoping words could dispel unwanted feelings, she asked, "Where did you learn to dance like this?"

"I grew up with two sisters," he said, guiding her

off the dance floor and picking up her cane. "For years, Keelin practiced on me, then if I didn't give Flanna a spin, she threatened tears. More than any young man can tolerate. A woman's tears, that is."

The way Curran was looking at her again...Jane quickly averted her eyes.

Perhaps the connection she'd felt had been all in her head, but she was taking no chances. A private person, she felt certain that knowledge was better kept to herself. If he searched deep enough, she feared he would expose her.

Expose the horrible thing she had done.

"You seem flushed. Perhaps a cool drink and some air?"

Not seeing her grandmother at the moment, she agreed. Perhaps the cool night air would clear her head, allow her some perspective. Curran led her out from under the tent to the shelter of a big tree and an empty bench, where he deposited her cane.

"You could sit while I get the drinks," he suggested.

She nodded but didn't make a move. Still caught by him, she could hardly think.

"Sheena—"

"Don't call me that!"

"You don't like the name?"

"The name is beautiful." Shivering at unwanted memories, she turned away from him and stepped into the shelter of the old maple. "But it's not me."

To her dismay, he followed, pressed her into the bark with his very nearness. He lifted a stray curl from the side of her face with one finger and toyed with it.

Gazing steadily into her eyes, he whispered, "You are beautiful."

"No, not when I—I'm damaged—"

"Only in your mind, lovely Sheena," he murmured, sliding his hand behind her head. "Only in your mind."

"That's the problem."

The feel of his hand on the sensitive flesh of her neck thrilled her. And yet she dismissed the promise of his touch. Not for her, she thought.

"I've been known to fix problems of the mind that no one else could."

"With horses, yes."

"Then perhaps 'tis time I expanded my practice to include another species," he said, his tone low and cajoling.

He gave her no leeway. No time to object. No time to push him away. He kissed her, devoured her, like a man who hadn't had a woman for too long.

Jane's arms wrapped around his neck of their own volition. Her body seemed perfectly capable of accepting what she couldn't. What her mind told her couldn't be.

This wasn't right. Wasn't for her. Wasn't real.

Hadn't she had enough of that?

But her body didn't know it wasn't real. Her body betrayed her will. Her flesh grew warm and supple beneath his exploring hand, first at the small of her back, then lower. She was alive as she hadn't been in a very long time.

"Oh, pardon me!" came the surprised voice of an elderly woman.

Whose words shocked Jane and drove her away from Curran. She might have fallen, but he snaked an arm around her waist as if it was the most natural thing in the world.

"Mrs. Sterling." Jane's heart was pounding against her ribs. Great. One of the biggest gossips in the area had caught them. "Nice evening."

"Nice for you, I see." The silver-haired woman peered at Curran for a moment through pop-bottle-thick glasses, before murmuring, "Ah, young lovers, so bold, so foolish. I didn't mean to interrupt." Though she backed away, she didn't take her gaze off them. "Go on with what you were doing."

Sensing Curran wouldn't mind, Jane muttered, "Don't even think about it."

Young lovers, indeed. The foolish part fit well enough. And now everyone would know.

Why had she agreed to come?

"Sit," Curran said again. "And I'll get you that drink. What would you like?"

"Lemonade. With vodka."

Not that a drink was likely to remove the sting of their discovery.

Watching him cross to the bar, she perched on the bench and waited for her senses to quiet. The only reason she'd complied was that it was less embarrassing to remain in the dark alone than to be seen on Curran's arm. That would just give the guests something more to buzz about. No doubt Mrs. Sterling was already circulating and spreading news of their tryst.

Still awkwardly perched on the bench, she breathed deeply and tried to calm the inner turmoil that threatened to swallow her whole.

What had she been thinking, kissing a stranger that way?

Hadn't she learned anything from experience?

Determined that she wouldn't repeat the mistake she'd made with Gavin Shaw, Jane focused on strengthening the barriers that would keep Curran at a distance.

SOMETHING TERRIBLE had happened to Jane Grantham. Curran knew that as well as he knew anything. For a moment, he'd experienced her emotions. Her physical pain. Nothing like that had ever happened to him before. Nothing had even come close with another person.

Then why Jane?

And how, when his gift had always been restricted to animals in the past, primarily to horses?

Questions continued to plague him as he crossed through the crowd, nodding and waving to horse people he knew. He had to stop for a moment, to shake another trainer's hand, but he was so distracted, the man promised to catch up with him at the track and let him go on.

He could put his connection to Jane to only one thing. Her bond with Finn mac Cumhail. He'd seen it with his own eyes, had experienced it when he'd watched them the day before. He hadn't understood it then, but he understood it now.

Shared pain.

No other explanation fit.

Which should have been obvious if he had been paying better attention, Curran thought. But his attraction to the lovely Miss Grantham had distracted him.

Shared pain, but of what? The questions went on. An accident, as she'd told her grandmother? He doubted it. The hurt to Jane's leg had been deliberate. And to Finn, Curran thought, remembering the placement of those scars—nose, shoulder and foreleg.

Just as if someone had beaten them both...

The incident had been so horrific that it had crazed them both, as well. Yes, Jane had become unbalanced to some extent, as he'd experienced for himself. Talking about it would help her resolve her anger and grief and whatever else she had undergone. But she obviously wasn't talking about the incident, at least not to Belle.

And he doubted that she would readily confide in him, either. Rather than bringing them closer, he guessed that the connection she'd recognized on the dance floor, added to the kiss, had pushed her away.

Curran arrived at the bar and gave his drink orders. He had just collected them when Mukhtar Saladin caught up with him and stopped him from getting back to Jane.

"McKenna, isn't it?" Saladin asked with a touch of displeasure to his tone.

The Saudi owner knew very well who he was— horses he'd trained had competed with several owned by the Arab, and some had even won—though Saladin had never deigned to speak to him before.

"Saladin. What can I do for you?"

"It is what I can do for you."

"And that would be...?"

"To warn you away from the Irish Thoroughbred. For your own good, of course."

Curran snorted. "I'll be begging your pardon on that one now."

"Working with Finn mac Cumhail could prove to be dangerous."

"For whom?" Curran carefully hid his outrage behind a smooth smile. "Me? Or you?"

"How would I be in danger?"

"You would be in danger of losing the Classic."

"That won't happen."

"You seem a tad too confident, lad."

Curran smiled inwardly when the familiar address brought a scowl from the other man, who obviously considered a lowly trainer less than his equal.

Curran hated nothing more than the class distinctions he still encountered in the business between wealthy owners and the people who made money for them. *Some* wealthy owners, he amended to be fair. Not everyone was a Mukhtar Saladin.

Or a Maggie Butler.

"Why shouldn't I be confident?" Saladin asked. "Stonehenge is the best horse I have ever owned."

His voice was raised just enough that ears eager for gossip became attuned to their conversation. People around them were staring. Curran could hardly blame them. An owner having a go at a trainer who didn't even work for him was fair fodder for the gossip mill. Racing was a small, closed community, after all.

Curran reminded him, "But Finn mac Cumhail beat Stonehenge the last time out."

"By a neck only. Besides, that crazed stallion is not the same horse he was then," Saladin argued. "And trying to bring him back could get you killed."

Curran's smile faded. "That sounds like a threat."

"A warning, as I said." Saladin straightened the lapels of his tux. "The horse has been maddened, and I merely meant that you take your life in your own hands by getting anywhere near him."

Was that what the Saudi owner really meant? Curran wondered.

Or did he need to start watching his back?

STRENGTHENING HER barriers—hah!

Every time Jane saw Curran in her mind's eye, something inside her softened a little instead. How could she not be attracted to him when he was so charming, so handsome, so passionate?

Perhaps a fool never learned.

On impulse, she rose and headed away from the tents and from the possibility of letting Curran get to her again. She had to take back control first. He would return with their drinks any moment now, and she would be far too vulnerable to face him.

The sparkle of moon-splashed water drew her. The wood-chip path wound down through a stand of trees that edged a pond where crickets and frogs called to each other. Perhaps a few minutes alone with nature would clear her hormones of a dubious attraction to a certain horse trainer.

Carefully, she started along the path, making sure her cane found solid ground before taking each step. Inclines were especially difficult for her since her knee prevented getting the feel of solid ground beneath her left foot. Not only had the joint been affected, but nerves, as well.

When the walk went smoothly, she breathed a sigh of relief, certain that this was exactly what she needed to gather herself together, so that she could face everyone as if nothing had happened.

Enough stares followed her wherever she went as it was, Jane thought. People wondering about the accident but too polite to ask for details openly.

Only the trainers had been at all direct with her, but they'd been interested in Finn's problems, not in hers.

She'd told them a version of the truth. That a worker had put a terrible scare into the stallion and that he'd been hurt in the process.

By their expressions, which had always hardened at hearing even the abbreviated story, she knew they'd gotten the awful picture without a blow-by-blow account. They, too, had avoided probing further.

A sound like a footfall behind her made Jane whip around and almost lose her balance.

"Curran?"

No answer.

Jane squinted but saw no movement through the trees. Probably a small animal foraging for food, she decided. Turning carefully, she continued.

Curran McKenna was another story. He wasn't too polite to probe. He hadn't asked about her injury or Finn's, not in so many words. Not yet. That was coming, she was certain.

And what she'd experienced on the dance floor, something she couldn't quite put words to, still shook her.

Shuddering despite the warm night, Jane rubbed a sudden chill from her arm.

And as she approached the water's edge and the fragile-looking bridge that crossed the pond, another sound, this one definitely a footfall, she was certain, made her turn again.

This time she said naught, simply stared into the stand of trees illuminated by a full moon.

Expecting to see Curran pop out at her, she grew

fidgety when nothing of the sort happened. Her pulse picked up and a weird feeling skittered through her.

"Curran?" she murmured, slowly backing up.

Her hand tightened on the cane. She was having trouble breathing.

Nothing there, she told herself as one foot hit boards that creaked, then the other. *Your imagination.*

There was no reason to be afraid. What was wrong with her? Stupid question, she thought as the horror flashed through her mind. She couldn't rid herself of the savage memories that haunted her.

"Damn!"

She was imagining things. She had to stop this. She had to find a way to be comfortable in her own skin again. She was home now, among friends.

How much safer could she be?

A few more steps and she was about to refocus her attention on the bridge when a movement caught her eye. Even as she took another step, she whipped her head back and caught a man's silhouette between trees.

"Jane! Wait!"

She gaped and her eyes rounded as her cane slipped and her knee refused to hold her. The fragile rail cracked and gave way under her careening weight.

And the next thing Jane saw was the pond rushing up to swallow her.

Chapter Five

Curran dropped the drinks and ran, cursing himself for calling out to Jane and distracting her like that. He saw her head bob up out of the water, followed by the rest of her upper body. She was sitting on the bottom, sputtering. She was also moving like a turtle on its back. Apparently she was unable to get herself up.

By the time he reached the bridge, her sounds of frustration were punctuated by slaps at the water.

"You'll surely hurt the pond if you don't stop that battering." Not to mention herself.

"Curran!"

"Is it help you need, lass? All you have to do is say so."

"Yes," she said in a small, frustrated voice.

He reached a hand over the side of the bridge. "Grab on, then."

"Don't pull. I can do it myself."

"I believe you can, just as you do everything for yourself. But there are times when everyone needs a hand."

He held steady for her, an anchor, nothing more.

Maneuvering her bottom and her good leg into position, she managed to haul herself up to her feet.

"I apologize," Curran said sincerely. "I didn't mean to startle you into taking a dip."

"You?" She let go of him and smoothed her wet hair away from her face. "That was you who called out?"

"Aye. Who else?"

She shook her head. "No one, of course."

But he could see the confusion in her face, dripping with pond water. He wanted to reach out and brush the droplets from her cheek, but right now he didn't think she would appreciate any attention that appeared too personal.

"I'll just walk myself up the bank," she mumbled, grasping onto the bridge to steady herself.

Curran took a quick look around and spotted her cane. "Here," he said, fetching and offering it to her.

"Thank you."

A moment later, she was struggling out of the water and Curran was standing in front of her, once more holding out his hand. She gave him a suspicious expression before taking it. Again, he allowed her to do the work. He knew when to press his advantage and this was not the right time.

"What do I do now? Look at me. I'm a mess."

Actually, she appeared quite fetching in the moonlight with her hair disheveled around her face and elegant neck. A water nymph risen from the sea. Not that she would appreciate the analogy.

"Perhaps our hostess has some dry clothing you can borrow."

"Borrow? I don't want her to know this happened." She sounded horrified at the thought. "No,

I have to get out of here without anyone seeing me like this.''

"A little late for that."

He indicated the tented area. Several people were standing at its edge, pointing to them and waving over others.

"Oh, swell."

There was nothing for it but to follow the trail back up to the party. By the time they got to the bench area, Belle was rushing toward them.

"Jane, dear, are you all right?"

"Just a little wet, Nani," Jane said, smiling and trying to put a good face on the incident. "You know me these days. Just call me Jane 'Klutz' Grantham, the embarrassment of any social occasion."

"Jane, please stop doing this to yourself."

"Yes, I am responsible, aren't I," she said breathlessly, making Curran wonder what exactly she meant by that. He didn't imagine she was referring to the dunking.

"Jane—"

"Please, no lectures, not now, Nani." Her voice trembled a bit. "I just want to leave." Quickly she added, "But you stay and have a wonderful time. I'm sure one of your friends will be willing to give you and Curran a ride. If not, I can come back for you later."

"Mitzi does go right by our place on her way home."

"If you don't mind, then," Curran said, "I'll be leaving, as well."

Belle's shrug was resigned. "All right. You take care of my granddaughter."

Curran whispered conspiratorially in her ear. "She

would say she can take care of herself, but you and I, we know differently.''

Belle patted his arm.

Then Curran braced Jane and led her back to the tent. As they cut through the crowd, murmurs followed. Jane stiffened. Curran gave her arm a reassuring squeeze and kept the momentum going all the way to the car.

As they drove, she sat quietly in the passenger seat and stared out the side window.

For once, Curran didn't sense strong emotions emanating from her. She seemed hollow to him, as if she'd gone blank inside, nothing to read, as if she'd put herself on hold.

And no wonder.

An emotionally exhausting evening, one in which she hadn't wanted to participate, had become one huge embarrassment. Considering the way she felt about appearances, Curran supposed he could hardly blame her.

If only she didn't tie herself up in knots over what others thought...

That fact alone should distance him from her.

A thought that resonated until the moment he pulled up in her driveway and cut the engine.

''Thank you for seeing me home,'' Jane said as she fled the car.

''I'll see you inside.''

''That won't be necessary.''

''I want to.''

''And I would prefer to be alone. I'm certain you can find something to keep you amused in town, perhaps the local pub, if not in your quarters.''

His quarters rather than *guest house.*

"Yes, ma'am."

Both her choice of words and tone of voice put him in his place. Her back was already to him and she leaned more heavily on her cane than she had earlier.

"See you first thing in the morning," he called after her, willing her to turn back to him.

But she slipped inside without answering, without so much as giving him another glance.

Or another thought, he supposed.

As Curran headed for *his quarters,* he wondered how he had let himself get into a situation that didn't bear repeating. Not that he was enamored of Miss Jane Grantham.

A kiss was just a kiss, he assured himself.

Still, uncomfortable memories of Maggie Butler surfaced. A young widow, she had relied on him for more than his horse-training skills. Only not in public. She, too, had been of the ilk that appearances were everything. And how would it look if she arrived at social functions on the arm of her lowly trainer, who had yet to prove himself?

He'd been a man in love, and so he had told himself that one day she would want him as a companion for more than the bedroom, where they wore each other out every night, and most mornings, to boot.

But the day that he wasn't required to sneak back to his own quarters before the housekeeper showed up never arrived.

And when he had pressed the issue of their being together out in the open, Maggie had simply fired him. It had been that simple to her if not to him. To his everlasting regret, he'd fallen madly in love with the woman.

And she had him off her property for good barely a day after he had withdrawn Finn mac Cumhail from the Irish Derby because of a pulled tendon.

The twin disappointments had troubled him ever since.

Upon entering the guest house, the first thing Curran did was to check the answering machine for messages, but the red eye wasn't blinking at him this night.

Wanting to put himself in a more congenial mood, he decided to call his sister Keelin, who had lived in the Americas for the better part of three years now. He meant to visit with her and her family in Chicago a while before heading back for Ireland.

"Curran, 'tis grand to hear your lovely voice," was the first thing his beloved sibling said.

"And yours. What's that I hear in the background?" A familiar scream, he thought. "It wouldn't be my niece, Miss Kelly McKenna Leighton, would it now?"

"That it would," Keelin said with a laugh. "She and her cousins are up to mischief as usual."

"The triplets are there?"

"Aye. Have you ever heard the expression *terrible twos?* Well, multiply that by four this evening. Tyler and I are baby-sitting so that Roz and Skelly can have a real night out," she said of their cousin and his wife. "Not to mention a bit of romance. When I say Tyler and I, by the way, that's meant to be taken with a pinch of salt. But his daughter Cheryl makes up for my husband's lackadaisical attitude. He just wants to play with the children and leaves the rest to us. So Cheryl is trying to round them up for bed even as we speak."

Taking the cordless phone and starting up for his bedroom, Curran said, "It must be grand."

"Rounding up four two-year-olds for bed?" Keelin sounded horrified.

"Nah, nah, don't get your knickers in a twist. I meant *having* them. Having a family. Someone to love and make babies with."

A moment of silence was followed by Keelin's "It *is* your turn, you know."

Understanding that she was referring to The McKenna Legacy, he stopped two steps from the landing. "In case you haven't noticed, the day has come and gone."

"And there is no new woman in your life?"

"Not of the romantic kind," he hedged, resuming his route to the bedroom.

"Now why, boyo, am I not believing that? How old is this Jane Grantham?"

"Late twenties."

"And what is she like?"

"Afraid."

"Of?"

"Everything. Appearing foolish, mostly. And something dark that she won't talk about."

"What is it, Curran? That strangeness in your tone. Tell me."

He sighed. He never could hide anything from Keelin. "I'm able to read her."

An intake of breath told him the shorthand was all his sister needed. She understood. This was the real reason he had called her, Curran suddenly realized. Because he could tell her anything and she would understand. Though her gift was different than his—

she could see through the eyes of a person in trouble—she, as they said, *got it.*

"How?" she asked.

"Her connection with the stallion." Kicking off his shoes, he threw himself on the bed and stretched out. "Whatever happened to make him go mad happened to her, as well."

"What have you seen?"

"Not much. Blood. A weapon, perhaps." And the most startling fact of all. "I felt her pain when her leg was damaged. Literally."

Silence at the other end. Curran gave Keelin time to think on it.

When she spoke, the timbre of her voice had changed. "And you feel no attraction to this Grantham woman whatsoever?"

His hackles went up. "I'm drawn to her yes, but it's merely the circumstances!"

"You needn't be defensive with me, Curran. I am on your side, remember."

"Sorry. It's just that I get caught up in the moment, and then later, when I think about it..." He left the statement unfinished.

"Exactly," Keelin said.

"Exactly what?"

"You must be careful, Curran. There are forces at work here more powerful than you can imagine. I know this from experience. Mine. Skelly's. Kate's. Donovan's."

"What exactly are you going on about?"

"Your fate, brother dear. Whether or not you are willing to admit it yet, you have indeed met her."

"You're full of the blarney, Keelin."

"Am I? Something special lies between you and

this woman, Curran. You know that as well as I. Why else would you have the connection?''

''I told you, because of the horse.''

''I know what you said. But what do you feel?'' When he didn't immediately answer, she said, ''That's what I thought. Accept it, then, Curran—not only is Jane Grantham your legacy, but unless you somehow escape it, terrible danger awaits you both!''

KEELIN'S WARNING echoed through Curran's dreams and, when he awakened, stayed poised at the back of his mind. He knew the stories that defined his grandmother's legacy. Each of the other McKenna cousins who had reached his or her thirty-third birthday had come close to crossing over to the other side and being rejoined with their Grandmother Moira.

Hadn't Finn and Jane been involved in a dangerous situation already? One that could pull him in and prove to be the danger that Keelin feared.

But Jane Grantham—the love of his life?

He just couldn't feature it, not after the way she'd dismissed him the night before.

And so, when he approached the appointed time to meet Jane at the barn, Curran found himself dragging his heels. A bit of fun and flirtation with the woman had been one thing. What Keelin was suggesting was something else altogether. Still, when he saw Jane, he couldn't deny that she called to him in some primal way.

Only now, rather than being captivated, he was irked by the knowledge. He wouldn't soon forget how she had reminded him of Maggie Butler.

Jane had beaten him to the paddock and was sitting on the chair he'd used the day before. And, just as he had, she was reading a newspaper. He chose to approach her with the briskness and professionalism of their relationship as defined by her.

"I won't be needing props this morning," he announced.

She lowered the newspaper and folded it. "I was merely trying to prepare since you are late."

That she noticed grated on him further. "By five minutes."

"Yes."

Jane managed to stand by pushing on the seat with one hand, the back of the chair with the other. He waited for her to fetch her cane, but it didn't seem to be nearby. Instead, she hung on to the back of the chair and took a step, moved the chair toward the fence and took another step.

"Here," he said, hopping the fence before she could continue. "I'll do that."

When he grabbed the chair back, their hands met. Jane faltered. As did he. The signals he was reading from her today had nothing to do with anger or fear and everything with the fact that she was a woman and he a man. No class division here.

Her letting go and pulling back her hand provided a major relief. He swung the chair to the outside of the paddock before realizing that she was still standing where he'd left her. Perhaps she'd needed the chair in lieu of the cane. Suddenly feeling mean-spirited about having removed it, he stepped toward Jane and offered her his hand. She gave him a puzzling look before brushing by him.

"I'll get Finn."

"Well, you're welcome, then," he muttered, watching her go.

Today must be a good day. Her gait was less pronounced, even after her fall from the bridge the night before. Or perhaps she was trying harder to save face. That seemed to be her greatest worry.

Other than Finn, Curran amended.

And it was Finn on whom he needed to focus, he reminded himself. So, by the time the stallion came prancing into the paddock, he had relegated Jane, and his sister's predictions, to the back of his mind.

He began by standing still and silent.

Finn skirted him and kept his distance. Curran waited a few moments, then walked away from the stallion. Finn watched him, his stance one of ready flight. In circling along the fence, Curran eventually came too close for Finn's comfort. He moved away, straight across the paddock.

"Come now, Finn, you have no reason to fear me," Curran wheedled as he made a second approach. "You remember me, now, don't you, lad?"

Finn snorted and trotted away from him again. Curran continued to stroll around and to speak to the horse, using his name often. Though he continued to have Finn's full attention, the stallion was still on guard.

Twenty minutes with no further success. Curran let it go and had Jane stable him.

But he proceeded on a regular schedule the way he had the day before, allowing Finn to relax and then having another go at him, miniconfrontations that quickly multiplied, so it was almost as if days rather than hours had passed. He wore the stallion down a bit at a time until, in the third effort, Finn stopped avoiding him.

When he realized the stallion was following him, if at a safe distance, Curran felt a moment of triumph.

Now, if only getting close enough to touch the stallion was an easier task than dealing with the woman.

THEY'D PICKED UP an audience, Jane suddenly realized halfway through the afternoon. Patiently waiting to speak to Curran on the opposite side of the paddock, Ned closely watched his every move with the stallion. Jimiyu Stams sat on the top board, seemingly entranced by the horse he was to ride. And Phyllis Singleton-Volmer was coming from the house.

A sick feeling welled up in Jane. She closed her eyes for a moment. Any second now, the woman would be all over her.

When that didn't happen, she peered out to find Phyllis at the fence several yards away, staring not at her but at the drama unfolding in the paddock.

Finn was inching closer and closer to Curran.

And while Phyllis wore a poker face, her body language told Jane that she was on edge. Why?

As if the society matron felt Jane's eyes on her, she turned. One blink and the carefully studied neutral expression welled into one of sympathy.

Here it comes, Jane thought.

"Oh, Jane, dear, I was appalled when I heard about what happened to you last night. I just had to drop by to make certain that you were recovered."

Exactly as she'd feared.

"I had nothing to recover from," Jane assured the woman, wearing her own poker face. "I just needed to climb out of those wet clothes."

"Well, I feel so awful," Phyllis said, placing her hand over her heart. "I must make it up to you."

A drama queen as always, Jane noted. "There's nothing to make up."

"Indeed, there is. I've been meaning to have the rail on the bridge fixed for months now, and it took someone getting hurt to force me to it."

"I promise you that I'm not hurt."

"Lydia's little girl injured because of me," Phyllis said, sweeping over Jane's denial. "Your mother would never forgive me."

"Mother doesn't hold grudges."

"Yes, you're probably right. Lydia always was a cut above the rest. But let me make it up to you, anyway. I know!" she said brightly. "You and Curran had to leave the party before you even ate. I shall take you both to dinner tonight at my club. My treat, of course."

"That won't be necessary."

"Oh, but I insist." And before Jane could object again, she said, "I won't take no for an answer."

Seeing that she wouldn't, Jane caved rather than make a bigger deal of the situation than it was. "All right. What time?"

"I shall pick you up promptly at seven." Phyllis enveloped her in a big hug and kissed the air next to her cheek. "Ciao, darling."

Mission accomplished, she strode off.

Leaving Jane to wonder what the visit really had been about. Phyllis had always been charming to her, but she'd never before sought out her company.

As if in tune with her thoughts, Curran asked, "What did our society hostess want?"

Startled, Jane turned to find him standing at the

fence. And behind him, Finn was practically sticking his nose over Curran's shoulder.

The quick progress stunned her and she had to stop herself from reaching out and trying to touch Finn's nose lest she reverse the gain. Possibilities once more tantalized her. Curran was turning Finn around so fast that it gave her renewed hope.

"Phyllis was very solicitous about last night," she said, a little breathless at the progress. "Whether we like it or not, you and I are being taken out to dinner to make up for the inconvenience."

"Hmm."

"Exactly. Phyllis has never shown any interest in cultivating me into her circle before, and I doubt that's the interest now. But indeed, she wants something," Jane mused. "And my guess would be it has something to do with you."

Chapter Six

The Lexington Pike Club felt almost like home, perhaps because it once had housed an extended family
before the patriarch had decided to sell the horse
farm.

The interior was pleasant, Jane thought. Exposed-
brick interior, period furniture, a fireplace that took
up half of one wall. Now renovated and added to,
the building boasted one of the best restaurants in the
area. Phyllis had preordered for them—prime rib and
lobster and a wonderful bottle of champagne. Jane
couldn't fault her taste, but again she held the
woman's generosity suspect.

They were halfway through their meal before
Phyllis turned the topic to the Thoroughbred Millions.

"Less than two weeks before the big race. I only
wish that I had an entry."

"But you do," Jane protested. "According to Mr.
Saladin, you convinced him to buy Stonehenge."

Her statement prompted her to wonder where the
Saudi owner might be tonight, after not wanting to
let Phyllis out of his sight the day before.

"Yes, but that's not the same as having my own

horse in the Classic,'' Phyllis rationalized. "Unfortunately, I've never had the resources to buy known horseflesh of that caliber, and I've never had the luck to stumble on an unexpected champion. Or to breed one. I've learned to content myself with an occasional Grade I victory.''

Jane didn't know Phyllis well enough to be aware of her financial interests. The woman owned a smaller farm than Grantham Acres, yet she both bred and raced horses. She also seemed to lead a wealthier lifestyle in general than the Granthams ever had, epitomized by the elaborate parties she threw during the racing season. Perhaps she went into debt to be the reigning socialite of the year.

Or perhaps someone else paid for her soirees—Mukhtar Saladin came readily to mind, as in years past did Richard Singleton and Harold Volmer, Phyllis's late husbands. Phyllis seemed always to hook up with older, well-to-do men with a passion for fine horseflesh.

"But you're not in the best of positions, either, Jane, dear, not with a half-mad horse,'' Phyllis said before turning her focus to Curran. "I understand the fate of Grantham Acres is resting on Finn mac Cumhail. It's a pity you can't get close enough to touch him, no less train him.''

"I feel that I'm making satisfactory progress in that direction,'' Curran said, leveling his gaze with hers.

"But time is running out.''

"Finn hasn't forgotten how to run, only how to trust. He'll be getting that back soon enough, and then who knows?''

"Soon enough to win the Classic?''

"I'm betting on it," Curran said. "Heavily."

Though Phyllis's "I see" was clipped, her smile didn't falter. "So what is your secret? Are you one of those mysterious horse whisperers or something?"

Curran's eyebrows shot up and his blue eyes held a definite gleam. "Or something. Though I do tend to speak softly around Finn."

"But what is it you tell him?" Phyllis persisted. "What is it that will make him yours?"

"I tell him what he needs to hear."

"But how do you know what that is?"

"Why, I read his mind, of course," Curran said with a big grin.

Jane wasn't smiling. He was acting as if he was joking, but she believed him. Is that what he'd been doing to *her* the night before?

Phyllis's laughter didn't quite reach her eyes. Suddenly she rose and snatched up her bag. "If you'll excuse me, I need to powder my nose."

As she rushed toward the ladies' lounge, Curran asked, "And you don't feel the need to join her? I thought women descended on the facilities in pairs."

"I thought I would give her a head start."

"Are you afraid she will corner you, then?"

"Even if she does, I can't tell her anything you haven't shared about your secret powers."

"Which seems to be the point of this evening."

"A fishing expedition," Jane agreed.

"I wonder if Saladin put her up to it."

"That would explain why he's not here tonight. Though what he thought you would reveal... something that would help him with Stonehenge?"

Was that the emergency that had pulled the Saudi away from Phyllis's party?

"Perhaps it was no more than finding out exactly how much a threat Finn might be," Curran said.

"Perhaps."

Thinking to find the ladies' room herself, Jane edged her chair back from the table. "If you'll excuse me, I'll give our hostess a chance to corner me after all."

Curran was quicker than she. He smoothly held her chair and, as she rose, braced her arm.

His touch was electric. Jane met his eyes and lost herself in the depth of his gaze for a moment.

As if their minds met on some level.

As if he was reading hers?

Jane couldn't get to the lounge fast enough. But once there, she composed herself before going inside. No need to give Phyllis any clue to what she might be feeling.

Calmly opening the door, she spotted the socialite perched on a chair before a mirror. But rather than primping, she was talking to someone, her cell phone to her ear.

"What do you mean it's not finished?" Phyllis was saying in a low voice. She didn't notice Jane coming up behind her. "You have no more..." Suddenly looking up, she met Jane's gaze in the mirror. She licked her lips. Then smiled. "Well, yes, darling, we'll discuss it later." She kissed at the phone, disconnected, then swung around to face Jane directly. "Ready to head for home?" she asked.

Jane was more than ready. She was also puzzled by Phyllis's demeanor. Her use of the endearment and the kiss...surely that had been Saladin on the other end. What could he have done to earn her ire? And did he really tolerate a woman speaking to him that way?

If Phyllis was stewing over something, she put on a good face all the way back to Grantham Acres. But when she let them off at the main house, she sped away without looking back.

His expression odd, Curran stared after her.

"That was a quick end to the evening," Jane said, relieved that it was over.

"The evening doesn't have to end."

"It's late and I have an early appointment in Lexington."

Now she had his attention.

"How early? What about Finn?"

"Meet me at the barn at seven-thirty and I'll get him out of his stall before I leave," Jane said, distracted by a noise coming from the main barn. She could swear that was a pounding like hooves against a stall wall. "You can just let him spend the morning in the paddock until I return."

"That'll do," he said. "Or perhaps he'll let me handle him. The appointment—anything I should know about?"

"A follow-up with my surgeon," she said, just as a loud squeal turned them both toward the barn.

Jane would recognize that sound in her sleep.

"Finn!" she cried.

"STAY PUT and I'll take care of it!" Curran told Jane.

Instinct drove him for the barn as fast as he could run. The thumps driving against wood were louder now, as was the terrible equine uproar of rage and fear. He immediately concentrated on the sounds but when blackness threatened his mind, he stopped trying to connect with Finn. He couldn't do anything for the horse if he was tossed back into the void created by his gift.

Throwing open the door and flying into the barn past mares who kicked their stalls and nickered at him, he realized the building hadn't been locked, nor did the alarm go off. Someone must have tampered with the security system.

And with Finn.

His stall door stood open and he was loose at the far end of the barn, twisting and bucking some invisible demon.

"Finn," Curran called in a soothing voice, even as he looked around into the dark corners of the barn for anything amiss. "What's the game, lad? Why are you so terrified?"

The sound of his voice got to the horse, who slowed his frenzy to a few halfhearted bucks.

"That's the lad. Quiet now, quiet. You're safe. 'Tis me here, is all."

Not quite. Footsteps behind him made him glance back to see Udell and Jimi Stams near the open barn door. Wide-eyed, father and son stood frozen to the spot. He indicated they should stay where they were.

"It's just Udell and Jimi," Curran murmured, pulling closer, praying that whatever had just happened hadn't undone the day's work. The horse had been coming along so well. "You know them now, Finn. Quiet, lad, quiet."

One last buck and Finn stopped thrashing. Snorting, he threw up his head, but when Curran inched forward, the horse's flesh quivered as if he'd been touched by a hand.

"Easy, Finn," Curran murmured as he drew even closer. Slow. Careful. No sharp movements. "There's a lad. You stand quiet or I might be desperate and then I would have to sing to you again."

A quick look at Finn's stall showed a decisive amount of damage but no broken latch. Someone had simply opened his stall door.

"Finn!"

The soft feminine cry pebbled the skin along Curran's spine. Jane flew past him, her limp pronounced, and went straight for the stallion.

"Don't be foolish now," he said, following her.

"Oh, Finn." The threat of tears filled her voice. "What happened to you this time?"

And before Curran knew what she was about, Jane wrapped her arms around the horse's neck and sobbed.

"Jane, he's all right," Curran said, placing a reassuring hand on her shoulder.

Reality shifted so quickly that he was instantly paralyzed, caught in a world not of the moment.

Wind and the rush of water pulled him along through the mist of his mind.

Crack! *Pain felled him.*

He looked up...a raised weapon crashed down, splitting Finn's nose...blood everywhere.

You're a ruined man! No one will ever let you near a horse again!

The words echoed through his head as he scrambled back, away from the threat. From the rage of a man too drunk to be steady on his feet.

He fought his way out of the mental maze...

Suddenly, he was thrown back into the moment.

Still holding on to Finn, Jane was staring at him aghast. She knew. She definitely knew.

He shifted focus to the stallion, who seemed to have calmed as if by magic. Because of him? Because of Jane? Or was it the connection between them all?

"We need to check him," Curran said quietly.

"And then we need to talk."

"Indeed."

It was more than time for some disclosures, though Curran wasn't looking forward to it. At least not the part where he had to explain himself.

"Miss Jane, what can we do to help?" Udell asked.

As if the burden of the world were resting on her shoulders, she looked to Curran.

"In the morning, you and Jimi can see to repairs," he said, indicating the stall. The one opposite was empty and usable with the addition of hay, water and feed. "Right now, set this one up for Finn. And one of us needs to watch over him through the night until we can have someone out from the security company to see why the system failed. We can take shifts."

"No, I'll do it," Jimi said. "I'll bring a cot in and sleep outside Finn's stall. I've done that dozens of times with pregnant mares due to deliver. Don't worry, I'm a light sleeper. No one's gonna get by me."

"I didn't mean to put it all on your shoulders, lad."

"If I'm gonna ride him in the Classic, then he's gotta get to know me better."

Curran only hoped Jimi Stams was as good a rider

as Jane made him out to be. Considering how little time they had, they needed a jockey with a heart for this horse.

Father and son went to fetch a bale of hay while Curran and Jane checked over Finn to make certain he hadn't hurt himself. To Curran's amazement, Finn allowed his touch with little more than an ear flick and a snort.

Something had happened between the three of them, he realized. They had all connected. Even Finn.

People believed that animals operated on a more basic mental level than humans. Curran often found them to be more intuitive. And wasn't this proof? As if the stallion *got it,* Curran realized. As if Finn understood Curran's gift and therefore accepted him.

For suddenly the stallion allowed his touch at least as readily as he did Jane's. A definite improvement, possibly days ahead of schedule.

To add to the plus side, Finn hadn't suffered a new injury. Curran left the horse under Udell and Jimi's care with a clear conscience.

As he and Jane left the barn, he said, "Shall we have that talk now?"

"I'm certainly not in the mood for sleep," she whispered harshly.

Her voice was tight, Curran noted. Then, again, he wasn't looking forward to this dialogue either, as necessary as he knew it to be.

"Then let's go to my place," he suggested, "where we won't be disturbed."

He wanted to take Jane's arm, to support her, to make things a bit easier for her, but he suspected now was not the time to chance touching her. Instead, he adjusted his gait to hers. They walked side by side in silence as they crossed the barnyard and took the path to the guest house. Once inside, he bade her sit while he poured two bourbons over ice, suspecting that they would both need a bit of fortification.

One sip and she asked, ''What magic is it that you practice, Curran?''

''Not magic.'' He took the chair opposite her, a solid pine coffee table offering a sea of separation. ''Not anything I sought out. A gift. Part of my legacy from my grandmother. Moira McKenna was a special woman. A healer. A visionary. She knew things no one else did and helped those in trouble. She didn't ask for her gifts, not any more than I did mine.''

''What exactly is this gift of yours?''

''Some would say that I'm empathic.''

''You can read minds?''

''Emotions. Of Thoroughbreds, mostly.''

She shook her head. ''No, Curran. I felt you. I'm not crazy. I know something happened between us two different times that I can't explain.''

''Three,'' he amended. ''It started when I first saw you working with Finn the other morning. You fell...I didn't know if it was you or Finn...but it began then. We're all three connected by it.''

''I—I don't understand. It?''

''Shared pain,'' he explained. ''I've connected with your emotional pain perhaps because whatever happened to Finn happened to you as well.''

He didn't explain his sister Keelin's theory about why he'd been able to connect with her. He wasn't about to tell a woman he'd kissed once that she was his forever when he didn't more than half believe in The McKenna Legacy himself.

And he was reluctant to put words to the danger part, though it seemed Keelin had been right about the fates being set in motion. If the barn break-in was any indication of the forces at work, then none of them was safe.

"So you can what?" she asked, obviously struggling with the concept. "Connect with anyone you touch?"

"Animals, usually. But I've never been able to read another human being, not before you."

He could see she was trying to take it all in. A lot for her to handle. Even if she believed it.

"What was it that you saw?" she asked.

"Someone deliberately struck you in the knee. And Finn. You were trying to protect him."

"You could have made that assumption after seeing us together for the past few days." She shook her head, as if trying to convince herself. "It doesn't mean anything."

"It was night and the winds were high. It was near water, a river perhaps?"

She answered his question with one of her own. "What did the man look like?"

Curran shook his head. "I couldn't see him. I only felt him. His drunken rage."

"I'm still not convinced."

But she was white-knuckling her glass as she finished her bourbon, Curran noticed. She was open to the possibility even if she demanded proof.

He set down his own drink, leaned forward and gave her his best shot. "You told him that you would ruin him. That he would never work with another horse."

"My God," she breathed, letting go of her glass,

which tumbled to the carpet unharmed. Not that she seemed to notice. "What else?"

The way she was looking at him...

The face of desperation, Curran thought. She didn't want to be alone in this nightmare of hers. She didn't have to be if only she would trust him.

"Nothing more," he said. "That's it."

Now avoiding his gaze, she said, "I need to get back."

"To what? Refusing to talk about what happened won't free you."

Her expression closed and she started to rise, then suddenly noticed the glass. She picked it up from the floor and placed it on the table.

"Nothing will free me, not ever. Certainly not sharing the sordid details."

A peculiar way of putting it, he thought. "Try."

"I can't."

"If you can't do it for yourself, then think of Finn," he said, playing on her obviously active conscience. "Someone tried to harm him tonight. The same man?"

"That would be impossible."

"Why?"

Jane Grantham turned her back on him and started to leave. Determined to stop her, wondering what he was missing, Curran tried again.

"Jane, we all may be in danger here. How can you be so sure that the man who hurt you and Finn hasn't returned to finish the job?"

She stopped, and when she turned her face toward his, he saw an infinite sorrow reflected in her expression. Her eyes glassed over as if she was about to cry.

"Because he's dead," she said.

"How can you be sure?"

"Because I killed him."

With that unexpected confession, she left him staring after her.

Chapter Seven

That she'd said the words to another person at last should have made her feel better, Jane thought as she stripped and stepped into the shower. So why didn't they? Where was the relief that was supposed to come with confession?

Then, again, she had confessed already, to the Hudson Valley authorities in New York where the horror had happened. They'd believed her story and had sent her home to Kentucky, at least for the time being. But she would never truly believe it was finished. A person couldn't take another's life without consequences. And so far, there had been none.

At least none that she knew of.

Perhaps she would have to tell it all to lighten her soul. To stop seeing Gavin Shaw when she came into a room...or turned a corner...or stepped onto a bridge with a rotting handrail. Indeed, she had thought she'd seen someone in those trees the night before and that someone had been a dead man. A ghost who haunted her.

Would she never be free of him?

And if people knew the truth...she wasn't ready for that, certainly not with Curran McKenna. He was no confessor. As a matter of fact, he was as far away from being an uninterested party as was possible.

Or so it seemed.

Hot water pounded at her shoulders and back, but it didn't relieve her tension.

Curran was too interested in her. And getting too close. And she was letting him.

Was she not capable of learning from her mistakes?

Beyond that, she wanted to understand what was *really* happening between them.

Having felt it for herself, she couldn't deny the connection of which he spoke. But why her? Physical attraction seemed too simple an answer.

Curran McKenna made her distinctly uncomfortable. Part of her wanted him to be gone with the sunrise. But another part of her—one that had nothing to do with Finn and everything with herself—longed for him to get closer in a way that defied analysis.

For a moment, she closed her eyes and gave in to the fantasy of physical attraction. Curran's hands stroking her...his mouth exploring her...his bringing fire and a promise of forgetfulness to her very center...

But the fantasy was fleeting.

She couldn't lose herself in it. She couldn't hide from reality.

Jane turned off the faucet handles, stepped out of the shower and wrapped a huge bath sheet around her.

The bathroom mirror was steamed over and she could barely see her own reflection. The fog reminded her of the mist rising from the Hudson River that fateful night. Then the fog began dissipating, and she saw herself clearly, flushed with warmth, wet hair waving over her shoulders. Not unattractive when the disfiguring reminder was hidden.

Until she stepped back and removed the towel.

She let her gaze drop along the mirror, slowly, until she could see the reflection of the knee. It didn't even seem like *her* knee anymore. The joint was swollen and half-mooned by an angry red scar.

No simple arthroscopic surgery for her. No simple solutions. No full recovery.

No going back.

Dr. Daniels had assured her, however, that her scar would fade with time, as if that alone should make her feel better. And more than once when she had despaired, he'd shaken his head. It was, after all, only a knee.

Jane was certain that he had patients who were far worse off. But this was *her* knee and its near destruction had changed *her* life forever, and not just physically.

While the scar would fade with time, it would never disappear. She would always be aware of it, aware of the numbness where the nerves had been destroyed. Aware of the numbness inside herself. The scar would forever be a souvenir of her own foolishness and would dig as sharp as any knife.

To see it would remind her of her own culpability.

No one to blame but herself, Jane knew, vowing never again to allow herself to be so deluded.

"YOU'RE BEING UNREASONABLE," Susan complained over breakfast the next morning when Jane wouldn't agree to the teenager's plans for the evening.

"And you're making me late."

Added to which, she'd now lost her appetite.

Just what she needed, another fight with her sister when she was trying to get to an early doctor's appointment. It was as if knowing that, Susan had picked this very time to make her crazy, Jane thought, abandoning her eggs and bacon. And Nani sat there, pretending not to hear. The least her grandmother could do was back her up.

Susan tried again. "You haven't even met Tim."

"I don't need to meet him. You're a teenager, for heaven's sake, and he's an adult."

"He's not that much older."

"Anyone over twenty is too old for you!" she snapped.

"You're not my mother!"

"You're right." Jane lost her temper. "If you want me to, I can arrange for you to join Mother in North Carolina. Then you can be her headache instead of mine."

Susan pushed away from the table. "I hate you! Just because you had an accident that crippled you, you want everyone around you to be as miserable as you are."

"Susan!" From the head of the table, Belle finally spoke up. "That was out of line."

But was it true? Jane wondered, horrified at the accusation. If so, then she was appalled with herself.

Susan ran from the dining room. A moment later, the front door slammed.

Jane set her flatware on her plate as Melisande came in to start clearing.

"Jane, dear, have you really forgotten what it's like to be young?" her grandmother calmly asked her.

"You think I should let a seventeen-year-old go out with some trainer's assistant?"

"No, of course not. We're in agreement about that. She should be seeing boys from her high school, of course. But I think you could have handled the situation differently so that Susan wouldn't have been so volatile. The old Jane would have known how to do that."

"The old Jane is gone for good!" Irritated anew, she added, "And maybe the new Jane should go, too."

"Seeing that one disappear wouldn't be any loss," Melisande said with her typical frankness. "You have a problem on the farm, you fix it, no question. Why can't you try to do the same with yourself?"

Jane struggled up from her chair and glared. But the housekeeper merely stared her down.

"Jane, please, Melisande has a point," Belle said. "Let's talk about whatever has been bothering you."

Her grandmother being the one person she definitely could never confide in—she just couldn't let her down so horribly—Jane grabbed her cane and hurried out of the room. Neither woman tried to stop her, though she imagined they continued talking about her behind her back.

By the time she reached the barn, however, she was feeling guilty. Susan might be out of line, but not Nani. And not Melisande. Unfortunately, they only wanted to offer help where there was none to be had. And her doctor's appointment put her on extra edge, as usual.

She checked her watch. Seven twenty-six.

So where was Curran? she wondered, going inside to look for him.

Seemingly asleep on a cot outside Finn's temporary stall, Jimi sat up the moment the mares warned him of her approach. "Miss Jane. Anything I can do for you?"

"Take a break, Jimi. Eat. Get some *real* sleep," she told him. "Or you'll be too exhausted to be good to anyone, including Finn."

"Yes, ma'am. But first I'll get some chow. What time you want me back here?"

"That'll be up to Curran. Just keep your father informed if you leave the property."

Alone with Finn, then, Jane wondered if she was imagining it or if there was a subtle difference in the horse. He seemed more relaxed.

She opened the paddock door and then started blocking off any escape route.

"You shouldn't be doing anything that could get you dirty, dressed up for town as you are," Curran said as he entered the barn.

"If you would have been here—"

"I'll not be taking any guff from you on that score this morning. I took you on your word about being here at seven-thirty. If you had wanted seven-twenty or seven-ten, then you should have said so."

That he was right didn't put her in a better mood.

Huffily, she stood back and allowed him to finish blocking the aisle, after which he sauntered out into the paddock.

"Any time," he told her.

For once, the moment Jane opened his door, Finn ambled out of his stall and straight into the paddock.

She noted he immediately looked for Curran, and while he stretched his long legs by trotting around the perimeter, he didn't let the Irishman out of his sight for a second.

Undoubtedly, she was no longer needed here, Jane thought, leaving in something of a snit. She could be halfway to Lexington by now.

Not that she was anxious to see her surgeon. She didn't even know why she kept making appointments since, according to him, she was healed. Perhaps the flesh where he had cut her was healed, but that didn't mean she could walk without pain or that she wasn't still raw inside.

Indeed, the appointment depressed her further, with him verifying that her left leg would never be straight because the kneecap couldn't slide up over the joint with so much of the meniscus missing. If she were willing to consider further surgeries, however, they could remove some of the good cartilage, grow it in a laboratory, then implant plugs that could eventually grow together and replace the missing meniscus.

If it worked.

If she could spare the further recovery time to try.

Of course she said she would think about it.

If she couldn't do her job on the farm, who would take care of Grantham Acres? Nani did her best, but she had slowed down so much the past few years. And they couldn't afford to hire a farm manager. As it was, they were working short-staffed.

But at least the cartilage replacement was a possibility, she told herself as she finished dressing. Something to think about in the future, once their fates were decided.

She limped back into the reception area where she dutifully made her next appointment as ordered by the doctor. Waiting for the young woman to write the date on a card, Jane caught a voice with a familiar inflection drift toward her.

"So this Dr. Daniels, he's the best orthopedic man around, then?"

The male voice with the distinctly Irish lilt came from around the corner where several upholstered chairs were set up for patients. Jane's pulse immediately began to race as she thought she recognized it.

"He fixed my hip up right fine," an elderly woman said. "You need a new hip at your age?"

"Naw, not a hip. It's me hand."

Jane followed the voice around the corner.

"Had a wee accident back a few months, but National Health ain't all it's cracked up to be."

Her eyes widened when she saw the familiar fair-haired young man conversing with an elderly patient.

"Timothy Brady!" she gasped.

He started when he saw her, as well. "Jane Grantham. Imagine meeting you here."

He didn't sound all that pleased. She didn't blame him.

"What are you doing here?" she asked as he rose and moved away from the elderly woman and toward her. "In Kentucky, I mean."

"Working of course."

"For whom?"

Now that Gavin Shaw was dead…

"Holt Easterling. I'm his assistant now."

"Easterling," she repeated. "Mukhtar Saladin's trainer."

"Right." Expression intense, he asked, "Finn mac Cumhail—how's he doing?"

"Better," she hedged.

No need to tell the competition any more. He would repeat whatever she said to Easterling, who would in turn pass it on to Saladin. Better that they be kept in the dark as much as possible about Finn's progress. The Saladin team certainly wouldn't share a thing about Stonehenge.

"I would have sworn Finn was ruined after what happened in New York," he said.

"Well, neither of us did come out of that situation very well."

His gaze dropped to her cane. "I can see that. Finn won't be able to race in the Classic, now, will he?"

"That's what we're still hoping for."

"Susie seemed to think differently," he muttered.

"Susie?"

Jane frowned as the truth dawned on her. Timothy Brady was an assistant trainer…Susan's Tim! Her suspicions were immediately aroused.

Wondering if he had been instructed to use Susan to get information about Finn, she asked, "You do mean Susan Grantham, my sister, don't you?"

"Susan, then," Tim agreed. "I met her the other day at the track during morning workout."

Which sounded innocent enough on his part.

"At Churchill Downs?" Jane asked. "She was supposed to be in school."

"I can guarantee you she wasn't," Tim said. "She and her friends were there all morning. Ah, who would want to be taking some boring college course in the summer, anyway?"

"College? She told you that she's in college?

She's only seventeen!'' And she figured Tim Brady was twenty-five if he was a day. ''What are you thinking of, asking a girl that young on a date? I would appreciate your not encouraging her—''

''Whoa! What call do you have speaking to me in such a manner, and after all I did for you,'' he demanded, his expression suddenly angry. ''You certainly have a short memory, Jane Grantham.''

Jane took a deep breath. ''I apologize if I've misread you.''

Though she wasn't sure she had...

''No offense taken, then.''

An awkward silence hung between them until Jane said, ''Your hand, it's no better?''

''Not so's you'd know it.''

Tim flexed his fingers and she saw the bones in the hand itself didn't line up properly. Everything was a bit fuzzy, but she remembered Tim's hand had been bandaged when he'd brought the authorities to see her at the hospital. He'd said something about his having had an accident with a piece of machinery the day before. Only she hadn't remembered seeing the bandage earlier, when he'd found her and Finn after Gavin had tried to kill them.

''Tim, about the investigation,'' she said, feeling awkward. ''Has it progressed any?''

''I wouldn't know. I left Hudson Valley Farm shortly after you did. No reason for me to stay, after all, considering my employer was dead.''

''Why haven't I heard anything?''

''Could be there's nothing for you to know.''

She couldn't imagine the Hudson Valley police not contacting her in more than two months, but Tim might be right. Still...

"There's been no news of Gavin's death in the industry, either."

"Perhaps this is one scandal people are trying to avoid publicizing," he suggested. "And this isn't Ireland, after all. Not many people knew him here."

"But it's just odd, don't you think? Almost as if Gavin Shaw never existed, never made an impact on anyone's life."

Other than hers.

"If he had any family, it might be different."

Gavin Shaw had been alone in the world, a product of an Irish-Catholic orphanage, a background that he'd hated. Coming from a close-knit family herself, Jane understood his longing for a different life. He'd had a chance for that, but he'd ruined it. Even so, a man dying with no one to mourn him…no one to hold a memorial service for him…given the circumstances, she was inexplicably saddened.

"Well, Dr. Daniels is the best in this area," she assured Tim while making no guarantees. "I'm certain that he'll do his best to help you. Good luck."

Tim nodded. "To you, as well."

Jane left the office, feeling the weight of his gaze on her back.

An odd coincidence that of all the assistant trainers in the world, this one should show up on her piece of soil and in the employ of the owner of Finn's top competitor.

On the other hand, perhaps she shouldn't be suspicious, for she did remember Tim Brady's help well enough.

Gavin Shaw's assistant at that time, he had come back to the farm before daybreak and had found her and Finn in the field, damaged both physically and mentally. Tim had taken care of the horse. He had taken her to the emergency room and had brought the authorities to her. And two days later, after having made the travel arrangements for her and Finn, he'd seen her to her plane.

Seeing him again so unexpectedly had reopened the wounds.

What strange fate had brought them together again? she wondered.

CURRAN HELD the halter in his hands as he danced around the paddock with Finn. Encouraged by the leap in progress, he'd decided to push things along a bit.

Every time Finn came near him, Curran faced him squarely so that the horse would veer off, then be anxious to join him again. After which Curran changed tactics and began turning his back on Finn and ducking in a different direction, repeating the action until Finn was determined to get his attention.

That's when Curran stopped, his body at an angle to Finn, until the horse came right up to him and hung his nose over Curran's shoulder.

Curran held out the halter. Finn threw up his head and backed away and the game was renewed.

The second try was equally unsuccessful.

But on the third try, Curran changed tactics. He elevated his empty hand and touched Finn's nose.

A wave of longing, of suppressed fear...

Until he raised the halter in the other hand so that Finn could see it.

A shock of alarm threw him into the void.

His head restrained, he resisted as terror filled

him…as blows rained down on him…unable to move…unable to defend himself…

Curran didn't move. Instead, he concentrated on peaceful images and actions, his mental whisperings meant to calm the horse through his thoughts.

A big, open meadow, a small band of horses grazing…soft touches and an affectionate pat on the flank…him calmly and slowly tacking up the stallion while leaving him standing free…

Finn's turmoil quieted. He snorted and shuffled his feet but didn't move off.

"That's a lad," Curran murmured, stroking the horse, first along the tip of his nose and then up between his eyes. "You know I would never hurt you."

With that reassurance offered, he once more showed Finn the halter. Finn snuffled the leathers, and before the horse could change his mind, Curran slipped the halter up over his head and secured the buckle.

"See, not so bad."

He lightly hooked his finger in the cheek strap and moved forward slowly, Finn coming right along with him.

His moment of triumph didn't go unnoticed. As he rounded the paddock, he saw Jane standing on the lower fence board, staring.

To his own jaded eyes, her open, joyful expression made her the most beautiful woman in the world.

HIS DAYS were numbered unless he stopped making mistakes.

Next time he would take the tranquilizer gun. Checking to make certain no one was around to see him, he unlocked the cabinet and with a leather-clad hand, removed the handgun and several tranquilizer darts.

Of course, this way, he wouldn't be able to make it look like an accident. The tranquilizer would be in the horse's bloodstream. But at this point, what did he care what it looked like?

As long as he left no evidence, no one would be able to point a finger at him. And if anyone guessed, well, he would just slip back to his own country where, if anyone made accusations, he would deny everything and blame the crazy Americans.

A good plan, if only partially thought out.

After all, there was still Jane Grantham.

He shouldn't have waited so long, shouldn't have been so weak. Now she was rarely alone. McKenna was another matter—he didn't want a run-in with that one.

He'd seen her calendar. Knew her schedule. Hopefully, she would stick to it.

About to lock the cabinet, he removed a few more darts. They would be even more effective on a human than on a horse.

Effective enough to kill.

Chapter Eight

Throughout the afternoon, Curran continued to make progress with Finn. By the time they quit for the day, he'd taken Jimi inside the paddock to introduce him to the stallion. Finn didn't seem impressed with the teenage jockey who appeared in miniature when standing next to the Irish horse trainer. Jimi was probably five foot five and a hundred-fifteen when soaking wet.

Thankfully, Finn didn't get himself worked up at the intrusion of another human, not even when Jimi unthinkingly reached over and patted the horse's neck. Finn merely snorted and swished his tail, altogether normal behavior.

Jane began to believe that there was hope for Grantham Acres, after all.

"The security company was out this morning," Curran told her after they'd tucked the horse back in his new stall. "As it turns out, no one broke in. Whoever tried to get at Finn had the code."

"What? But the only people who know the code work here, and I trust them all."

"Maybe a slipped word over a pint—"

"No! I tell you, I know my people," Jane insisted,

now agitated. Jimi was still in the vicinity, fetching a treat for Finn, and she didn't want the jockey to overhear this argument and possibly be offended. She lowered her voice. "Anyone who is left has been with us for years. They worked for my father, for heaven's sake."

Taking the cue from her, Curran lowered his voice, as well. "How else could someone have gotten access to the damn code, then?"

"I don't know…" The image of the calendar on her desk opened to the wrong page hit her. "Curran, that first day when I found you in the farm office, had you been looking through my things?"

"You mean your desk? No."

"How about my day calendar?"

He shook his head. "Not that, either. I merely sat there, waiting for you to come find me."

"Then someone else searched my office. I found my calendar turned to the date of the Thoroughbred Millions and just assumed you had been browsing through it."

"Are you trying to tell me you wrote the code to the security system on one of the pages?"

She winced. "Guilty as charged."

"Well, it could have been anyone, then."

Her face bloomed with warmth. He didn't have to tell her it had been a careless act. But how could she have known that someone would actually be trying to get to Finn?

"I won't be writing down the new code where anyone can find it," she vowed.

"Plus, I had the security company set us up with a more comprehensive system. There's a camera installed outside, above the barn door and another in here.'' He pointed to a dark spot in the rafters. ''The monitor and recorder are in the guest-house den so that I can check things out from my quarters, no matter the time. The picture switches between the two cameras every few seconds.''

''That sounds good,'' Jane said, stilling her automatic reaction to the cost. A necessary expenditure, she told herself. ''We should be able to breathe easier at night.''

''Don't mean I'm not sleeping in the barn,'' Jimi said as he came back with a big apple for Finn. ''I got a shot at the Classic and I'm not letting anything happen to my ride.''

''Good lad,'' Curran said approvingly.

Jimi's face spread into a huge grin and he offered Finn the apple. The horse barely paused before lipping it out of his hand.

''I'll be back later,'' Jimi told Curran rather than her. Curran seemed to charm everyone around him, Jane thought. Nani…Finn…Jimi…

Her.

That troubled her almost as much as someone trying to get to their prized stallion. She didn't need her mind clouded by an attraction that wasn't going anywhere. Curran might like to take it to the bedroom, but he was bound for disappointment, she thought fiercely.

What she should be was grateful that she had another pair of eyes around the place. Another interested party and one ready to take charge if there were problems.

But…wasn't that exactly what she had been wishing for when she'd met Gavin Shaw?

As if he could read her mind, which Jane knew he

could at times, Curran said, "You know this thing would go easier if you could open up and talk to me, Sheena. Tell me what happened that night."

Her mouth went dry. She feared he wouldn't let it alone—or her—until he heard every detail. But she wasn't into sharing. Not that.

"I did tell you, Curran. I also told you not to call me Sheena."

"All you said was that you killed him. Him who?" he asked. "And how?"

Her pulse accelerated even at the thought of sharing the details. She shook her head and got ready for an argument.

"All right," he conceded, surprising her by giving in and turning his back on her. "We'll leave it, then." He started to walk away, but stopped long enough to say, "But when you feel the need to talk, you'll know where you can be finding a sympathetic ear."

Would he really be sympathetic? she wondered, almost tempted to give in and find out.

Jane willed herself to stand where she was until Curran was out of the barn.

More likely, he would see her for the foolish woman she had proved herself to be.

"So you'll be introducing me to himself tomorrow, then?" Ned asked over a pint of Murphy's.

Curran and his assistant had downed heart-unhealthy steak dinners at the local pub that had once been a stable, and were now sharing a pint.

"Tomorrow it is. After lunch. I want to get Finn used to one new person at a time, and Jimi will be in the paddock with me all morning."

"Riding?"

"I can't say yet. We'll see how it goes. But the sooner we get him used to people and Jimi on his back, the better," Curran said.

He was thinking they had a mere ten days until the Thoroughbred Millions when Holt Easterling entered the pub, followed by a fair-haired young man who looked familiar.

"That's Timothy Brady with Easterling," Ned said. "His new assistant."

"Easterling hired an Irishman?"

"Aye."

Unbelievable, as far as Curran was concerned. Normally, Easterling had only contempt for anything Irish.

"Where have I seen this Brady before?" Curran mused.

"I wouldn't be knowing that, Curran. Some Irish track, I suppose."

"That's it, of course. He must have worked for an Irish trainer before this. But which one?"

Ned said nothing.

Curran saw the Brit point to a table near the stone fireplace, which lay cold this summer evening. Tim Brady sauntered over to the table and flopped into a chair even as Holt Easterling made his way over to Curran.

"McKenna." He growled at both trainer and assistant. "Rumor has it you're going to put that mad Irish Thoroughbred in the Classic."

"Not up to me, now, is it?" Curran mused.

"You can stop it from happening."

"Why would I?"

"If for no other reason, to save face."

Curran laughed. "'Tis not *my* face that'll be needing saving."

"This time, Finn mac Cumhail won't come near Stonehenge."

"Then what are you fretting about?"

Easterling's complexion grew even darker. "Don't give me grief, McKenna."

"I'll be giving you whatever I want, Easterling," Curran stated, sitting up straighter. "First and foremost, a race that your English Thoroughbred won't be winning."

"Don't be so cocky. Stonehenge *will* win the Classic Cup for me. I shall do what I must to see to it."

With that, Holt Easterling strode over to his own table.

"Am I imagining it," Curran asked Ned, "or did that sound like a threat?"

THOUGHTS OF CURRAN distracted Jane all through her monthly meeting of broodmare farm owners.

The temptation was growing to tell him everything, when one of the men came over to her.

"Jane, someone just called to say your black mare got loose again in the back twenty acres."

Jane sighed. Just what she needed. "Who called? Udell? My grandmother?"

The man shrugged. "I didn't even take the message. I'm just passing it on."

"Thank you."

She called home, but when there was no answer, left a message on voice mail. Lord, she hoped Nani wasn't out there looking for Black Widow. It would be dark soon and the back acres could be treacherous. And not just to a human. She feared for the mare, who could easily break a leg in that area. She tried to get Udell, but no answer there, either.

Nothing for her to do but to see to Black Widow herself. The mare was young and thoroughly undisciplined. A good candidate for a mate to Finn when she came in season. The spicy mare had gotten out of her pasture more times than Jane liked to count.

The acreage was on the way home, so Jane turned her car off the pike and went in on a back road. She parked in the area most easily accessible, which wasn't saying much considering the land back there was hilly and chock-full of limestone rocks. She'd been able to manage it well enough in the past, when she'd been physically fit, but now...well, she wasn't looking forward to the experience.

With a cane in one hand, a flashlight in the other, she cut through a small wooded area and slowly went up a rise.

When she reached the top, she called, "Widdy!" She always used the mare's nickname. "Where are you, girl?"

As headstrong as the mare might be about getting her freedom, she was silly enough to always answer, as if she just couldn't help herself.

"Widdy!" Jane yelled, and whistled as loudly as she could, but tonight she got no answer. "Widdy!"

Twenty acres was a big parcel, and she was barely into it. A bit farther, she thought, flashing her beam around so that she could see where she was going. The moon was wedged behind a bank of clouds tonight. One wrong step and she could land in a ravine. That would be it for her.

"Widdy!"

Listening hard for any return answer, Jane was certain she heard a scrabbling sound from somewhere behind her.

"Widdy, you bad girl, is that you?" she called.

Spinning around in time to catch movement from the corner of her eye, she started. Her pulse triggered and she stared hard as she swept her flashlight over the stand of trees she'd just left. No horse in there, she realized.

A loud noise startled her. A crack. A shot? Someone was shooting at her! Her heart began to pound.

Which way to safety?

Another crack and something whistled close to her ear.

She didn't have time to think.

Clicking off the telling beam and taking flight, she could barely keep her feet under her. Her heart in her throat, she blindly traversed a ridge along a treacherous drop.

A third shot made her glance behind her just long enough that she skidded and was unable to catch herself. Losing her precious footing, she dropped the cane.

Then she panicked and reached forward to grab it...big mistake... Her feet shot out from under her and the next thing she knew, she was sliding down, down, down...

CURRAN WAS CHECKING the monitor in the den when he heard the banging at his front door.

"Coming," he said.

Assuming the visitor to be Jane, he was surprised to find Belle there instead.

"It's about my granddaughter," she said, her voice panicky. "Jane is in trouble—I know it!"

Immediately alarmed, Curran asked, "What kind of trouble?"

"I'm not sure. But she left a message on voice mail that she was going after one of our mares in the back acres because someone called at her meeting to let her know Black Widow was loose again. That area of the farm is really rough territory, and with her knee problems and all..." Belle shook her head. "Something made me check on the mare myself. Black Widow is still in her paddock."

"I don't understand."

Belle looked close to tears. "Neither do I."

Why the hell would someone send Jane on a wild-goose chase into an area that she wasn't prepared to negotiate in her physical condition?

Not liking the only answer he could think of, Curran said, "Don't worry, I'll find her. Just tell me how to get to these back acres of yours."

"I'll go with you."

"I'll be faster alone."

Belle accepted that, and as they headed for his rental car, she told him how to get to the back road.

It sounded like someone was out to get Jane, he thought as he drove off. But why?

He sensed it had to do with the "accident." And with the barn break-in.

Only Jane had the truth within her grasp, and he vowed that when he found her, he would make her come clean at last. She couldn't do everything on her own. She had to trust someone to help her and he meant that someone to be him.

THE WIND KNOCKED out of her, Jane lay facedown at the bottom of the ravine.

Whoever had been shooting at her was still up there. She was torn between getting to her feet and trying to find someplace to hide…and just staying where she was.

The scrape of leather against rock above decided her.

Heart pounding, fearing taking a simple breath, fingers digging into the rocky earth, she lay as still as death. That had to have been the shooter's purpose—to kill her. She would let him think that he had succeeded.

Was he staring down at her now, celebrating his success? She didn't dare look.

Her mouth was dry and she could hardly swallow. She didn't know how long she lay silent and unmoving before a clumsy footfall made her stomach cramp. Pebbles scattered down the ravine, some hitting her square in the back.

Sweat beaded her body.

How long? Jane wondered. How long would she have to play dead?

When she thought she couldn't tolerate it any longer, she heard the shooter move off, but still she didn't budge. She would outwait him, make sure that he didn't come back, that she wasn't fooled.

She relaxed enough to breathe, no more.

And though she continued to concentrate, to listen for sounds above her, she couldn't help wondering at the shooter's identity.

Who would want her dead?

What had she done to drive someone to this?

Only one possibility occurred to her…

From a distance, she heard a car start up. Still she stayed where she was.

Five minutes passed...ten...twenty...

Finally, she sat up and gingerly tested her body parts. All seemed intact. But her knee was hurting. Not the normal hurt from a good whomp, but that special hurt, like an abscessed tooth, a hot-wired nerve that wouldn't let up. All too familiar with that particular pain, she'd been grateful that she hadn't experienced it for some time. Now it was back with a vengeance.

Praying that she hadn't reinjured the knee, she turned over onto her good knee and attempted to stand. Stiff and sore, she awkwardly got to her feet and tested. Though the knee complained, it still seemed to be working.

Now what? No cane. No flashlight. And a wall of slippery earth and rock to ascend to get back to her car.

Jane felt like weeping. But tears would only hold her back, make getting out of this ravine more difficult. It would expend her energy and waste her time.

Crying could wait.

As if to give her a break, the moon slid out from behind the bank of clouds. But the minimal light merely emphasized the impossibility of her task. No getting around it, she had to climb more than a dozen feet up to the ridge.

Determining the easiest route—a path of sorts that snaked along the side of the ravine rather than straight up—Jane began, one step at a time. She leaned forward and dug her fingers into anything that would hold, whether rock or limb or root.

Slowly but surely, she edged upward and gradually a sense of triumph filled her.

Then a vehicle approached the area, the sound of its engine shooting right through her.

Nearly three-fourths of the way to success, she lost concentration and took a wrong step. The earth beneath her foot disintegrated. She slid down and landed on her knees. Then in grabbing for a handhold, she managed to rain pebbles and even rocks down on herself.

Big breaths, Jane told herself as stars lit behind her eyes again. *Take big breaths and the pain will pass.*

Lying against the incline, she feared she was finished, especially since the engine ceased and a car door slammed and she imagined the shooter had come back to finish the job.

Shaking and with a sense of desperation, she started upward again. Up and into the trees might be her only escape.

One step at a time…one handhold at a time. Fast…faster.

When she reached the top of the ridge, she was breathing hard, sweat slicked her body and the stress made all four limbs quiver.

Though unsteady, she was able to lurch forward, toward the trees. She almost had it when a bright beam from within the stand lit and caught her like a deer in the headlights of a car.

She was caught…

"Jane, are you all right?"

"Oh my God, Curran!"

He was at her side in an instant.

Realizing she was rescued, Jane threw herself against his chest, broke down and wept.

OVER HER PROTESTS, Curran picked her up in his arms and carried her back toward his car. Wiping away tears that seemed to come more from anger than injury, Jane was disheveled and filthy and probably bruised, but she was all right.

Fighting a growing rage at whomever was responsible, he pulled her closer to his chest and demanded to know, "What in the world possessed you to come out here alone?"

"Black Widow—"

"Is fine," he said. "Belle checked on her. You should have done the same before going off, half-cocked, into a dangerous situation."

She didn't argue with that. She didn't say anything until they reached the back road where he'd spotted her car. He set her down next to his rental and unlocked the passenger door.

"Wrong car," she said.

"You're in no condition to drive."

She dug into her pocket for her keys. "That's for me to decide."

"Not this time."

The moment she produced the key ring, he took it from her hand. Her expression of outrage was more than he could tolerate. Anything could have happened to her because she couldn't put her trust in anyone else.

"When are you going to learn that you don't always know best, Sheena?"

She already knew that. The mess with Gavin Shaw had proved it. Even so, she protested, "I'm an adult, entitled to make my own mistakes."

"Not when your life is on the line."

He appeared so fierce he made her stomach clench. And yet, she longed to feel his arms around her.

But when he took a step toward her, she panicked. "Don't—"

But he did. He cut off her protest by kissing her. Ignoring the odd taste of dirt on her lips, he tried to show her that she wasn't alone.

At first stiff in his arms, she softened and leaned into him. And while she didn't curl her arms around his neck as he might like, she did grab his shirtfront with both hands. Her tension came from something more dangerous than attraction, but perhaps she was trying to blot out one peril with the other.

Curran concentrated on calming her.

Conjuring images of a horse pasture filled with spring flowers, he held her hand and ran. Free of the cane, her knee and spirit healed, she ran with him.

Her tension eased and her grip on his clothing loosened, so he let himself back into the now.

Getting lost in each other out here where they were prey wouldn't be wise, so Curran ended the kiss, gently put her from him and indicated the passenger seat of his car.

"What did you just do to me?" she demanded breathlessly.

"Get in, Sheena."

Though her jaw tightened, she slid in without protest. Probably too much of an effort for her to fight him, Curran decided. Undoubtedly she would regain her sometimes savage tongue on the way back to the house.

Until then, he intended to press his advantage.

"How did you get this message about the mare getting loose?"

"One of the farm owners passed it on at the meeting. This particular mare had gotten loose too many times for me not to believe it."

"So, someone knew that and used it to get you out here alone. And from the looks of you..." He clenched his jaw. "What happened?"

For a moment, Curran thought she wouldn't answer. That he would have to add insult to injury to make her talk.

Then she said, "Someone just tried to kill me."

"Kill." His blood ran cold at her choice of words. "You'll be certain of that?"

"I'm sure someone was shooting at me. I fell down the ravine and I could hear him up above. At one point, he stood there looking down on me while I pretended to be dead. So, yes, I gathered that was his purpose."

"He, who?"

"I don't know."

Curran was talking more to himself than to her, when he said, "What could you possibly have done to make someone try to kill you?"

"Don't you think I asked myself the same question?"

"And the answer...?"

"I'm not sure."

At least that was a step away from *I don't know,* he thought as they pulled into the main drive. Not that she seemed in the mood to clarify.

Belle was waiting for them, panic written all over her face. She rushed out of the house and toward the car.

"I want to go to your place to clean up," Jane murmured, straightening her hair. "I don't want to scare her or Susan."

Belle was plenty frightened already, Curran thought as Jane rolled down her window.

"Jane, dear, you're all right."

"Of course I am, Nani." Jane reached out and patted her grandmother's hand. "You really didn't have to send in the cavalry. I'm fine, I promise."

"But...why would someone call you out on a wild-goose chase at night?"

"Bad sense of humor?"

Curran could see that Belle didn't buy it, but he was certain she knew challenging her granddaughter would get her nowhere.

"Listen, Nani, I'll be back to the house late. Curran and I have some strategies we want to discuss."

Belle looked to Curran.

"Don't worry, I'll take good care of her," he promised.

"All right, then."

Belle backed off, but Curran knew she watched after them as he pulled around the main house toward his quarters. Once there, he parked, then helped Jane out of the car and into the house.

When he turned on the kitchen lights, he got his first really good look at her. "You look as if you were mud wrestling."

"I imagine. I thought maybe I could shower and wash my clothes here so Nani doesn't see me like this."

"Why didn't you tell her the truth?"

"She's worried enough as it is. Plus, I don't even know the truth."

"I believe you do. Or at least part of it." Wondering what it would take to get her to open up to him, he asked, "Can you make it up the stairs to the bath?"

"I'll make it," she said, her voice tight.

"There's a robe on the back of the door. Meanwhile, can I get you something to drink?"

"Tea would be nice."

"Tea, then." He watched her limp toward the doorway. "How badly did you injure your knee?"

Pausing, she glanced over her shoulder at him. "I think the pain is far greater than any actual damage."

"Perhaps I ought to take a look at it. I've been doctoring animals since I was a lad." He couldn't resist adding, "And I do know a thing or two about a woman's body parts."

Despite the trauma she'd just been through, a smile trembled on her lips. "I'm sure you do."

Curran's groin tightened. He would like to be more familiar with *her* body parts and he was certain the thought had occurred to her, as well. As elegant as any Thoroughbred, she had an earthly quality that she tried to hide. But he recognized it, was drawn to it. Was drawn to her with her beautiful amber eyes that mesmerized him.

His grandmother's legacy might well be coming true, he realized, but now was not the time for such intimacies. Now the danger part consumed him, and he would have the truth before Jane left the guest house for her own bed.

Chapter Nine

Jane let the shower pour down on her until the hot water was exhausted. She shut down the faucet handles and grabbed a bath towel. No choice but to face the music, she thought, fighting a growing sense of dread.

Curran's scent clung to his bathrobe and whispered along her flesh as she slipped into it. Wearing a man's robe was about as intimate as one could get, other than indulging in the act itself.

She shook away the seductive thought before it could fully develop. Curran wasn't for her, and that kind of speculation would only land her in more trouble. Obviously, she was already in over her head.

From what direction the current danger came, she had no clue. If only she could be certain as to *why,* Jane thought, she might be able to figure out *who*.

She ran a comb through her damp hair, gathered up her dirty clothes and made her way back downstairs, taking one step at a time, hanging on to the banister for dear life. It suddenly occurred to her that losing her cane meant that Nani would want to know how.

"Your tea is ready."

The mingle of herbs and spices in the air greeted her as she touched down to the foyer, as did Curran, who stood in the doorway to the living room. Rather, he nearly filled it, she realized with a thrill. He leaned against the jamb looking more irresistible than should be allowed for a woman's peace of mind. His stance was nonchalant, as was the splash of dark hair that tumbled over his forehead. His right cheek dimpled in a smile.

Realizing she had forgotten to breathe for a moment, Jane gulped in some air and said, "I just need to throw these clothes in the wash."

"I can do that."

Curran straightened and started for her, but Jane put out a hand to keep him back.

"No, please. Stay where you are. I—I mean, I'll only be a moment."

Unfortunately for her, after that she would have no escape for more than an hour, until her clothes were ready. Hoping to speed up things, she put them on an abbreviated wash and single rinse, then with a sense of fate there was no escaping, joined Curran in the living room.

He'd thoughtfully set out a full teacup on the table next to the armchair with the most support, making it easier for her to sit and rise.

She'd barely settled herself in and taken a sip of tea when he said, "Don't you think it's time someone other than you and Finn knew the whole truth? From the beginning?"

Dressed in only his robe, she felt all too vulnerable and he was clearly pressing his advantage. She could hardly blame him, Jane thought with a sigh of resignation. And considering how involved Curran had become, he deserved all the weapons he could gather in his arsenal if he were not only to bring Finn around, but protect the horse, as well.

Besides, maybe someone else's knowing would make things easier on her.

"I assume my grandmother has filled you in on why I bought Finn mac Cumhail."

"To save Grantham Acres, yes."

"I'm not trying to pass the blame, but I actually got the idea from someone else."

"Who?"

This was the hard part—admitting how foolish she had been. She stirred a lump of sugar into her tea and sipped it. Anything to put off the inevitable. Curran patiently waited until she was ready.

Unable to avoid the truth any longer, she said, "He was an Irish trainer named Gavin Shaw."

"Shaw." Curran's inflection sounded odd as he echoed the man's name. "I know him."

Her pulse jagged, though she wasn't really surprised. Thoroughbred horse racing was a fairly small community and both men were from a tiny country. Still, she'd been hoping he might not even have met Gavin.

"Did you know him well?" she asked.

"For years, but we were no kith 'n kin."

Jane took a deep breath and launched into the story she'd been holding close.

"We met here in Kentucky last fall at the Keeneland meet. Gavin learned of our money problems and he suggested that with the right stud…"

She swallowed hard. Even though she'd turned everything over in her mind a thousand times, she could hardly fathom she'd brought this disaster on herself.

"Shaw recommended Finn?" Curran asked.

"He called me from Ireland last spring and told me about the stallion who was the perfect solution. The owner was about to retire Finn, but then thought he might make more money on his sale here in the United States, so he entered him into a Grade I race at Belmont. Gavin thought I could get a jump on the competition if I came to New York and expressed my interest in Finn personally before the race. He also said that he would be in New York, that he had rented a horse farm in the Hudson Valley for a few months."

"So he offered to make the arrangements."

"Yes."

She stopped there. How much did Curran really need? Jane wondered.

"Obviously, you agreed."

"To my everlasting regret." She decided there were some details he could do without. "He was renting a farm in the Hudson Valley. That's where we took Finn after I bought him. We were ready to come back to Grantham Acres in two days. But that night, my sleep was broken by terrified squeals coming from a distance."

"Finn."

She nodded. "I went out to the barn and then to the pasture. Finn was tied to a fence post and rearing to defend himself against Gavin, who was wielding that length of pipe. I was horrified." Even with her eyes open, she could see his distorted features as clearly as if they were before her now. "How could he do such a thing? I tried to stop him. But he was crazed himself that night. Drunk. Desperate…"

"And you were injured trying to protect Finn,"

Curran said. "You threatened to ruin Shaw and he turned on you. He would have killed you to protect his reputation. That's it, isn't it? So you defended yourself. How?"

"With a pitchfork," she whispered, the vivid images continuing to flood her. "I thought it would keep him back…but the next thing I knew, he was staggering away from me and pulling the tines from his gut. So much blood. He tried to hold it in, but it squished through his fingers." She shuddered at the memory. "He fell back against the fencing and it gave under his weight. We were on a bluff, high over the Hudson River. His scream as he fell still echoes through my head."

Curran didn't speak and Jane shook inside. Would he condemn her now? Even as she had condemned herself every day since the horror had happened?

But all he asked was, "What did you do then?"

"Nothing. I couldn't do anything. I tried to get up, but my knee wouldn't support me. And the pain…I don't know how long I lay there, hearing screams over and over in my mind. Finn's. Gavin's. My own. Eventually Timothy Brady found me. He took care of everything. The horse…me…the authorities."

"Timothy Brady," Curran echoed, a start of surprise in his tone. "He works for Holt Easterling now."

"I know. I saw him at the doctor's office this morning. So strange," she murmured. "If Gavin had not betrayed us, Timothy would be working to ready Finn for the Classic. Instead, he's working against us."

"An interesting way to put it," Curran mused.

Getting his point, she said, "No, I didn't mean it that way!"

"Why not? How do you know Brady wasn't out there taking shots at you tonight?"

"Because he helped me. He even brought the police to the emergency room."

She could still see them, too, one pacing the hallway, the other taking her story.

"You'll not be under any charges, I assume."

"After investigating, the authorities were satisfied with my story, although they didn't find Gavin. The current must have pulled his body miles downriver. Without a body...well, Gavin was considered missing rather than dead. They told me they would keep up the search. I was to return to Kentucky as planned with Finn and they would contact me with further developments."

"But they never did."

"No."

"Odd. Why would the authorities have encouraged you to leave the area without a more complete investigation?"

"I'm sure the investigation is continuing."

"But it has been months and they haven't even contacted you. Something isn't right here, Jane. We both know that after what happened to you tonight. There's more to this story than you realize. It sounds as if there's a cover-up going on."

He had a point, one she hadn't wanted to examine too closely. Yet she had to. Her life might really be on the line.

"Why didn't you ever tell anyone the truth?" he asked. "Don't you think Belle deserves it?"

"Has anyone ever died because of you?" she

snapped. "Gavin is a burden on my soul and always will be. The Hudson Valley police kept the story hushed, away from the media, for which I am very grateful. Why would I want to perpetuate it?"

"So, only a few people know what happened. You. The authorities. Timothy Brady."

"And now you." She sighed. "Maybe I handled this whole thing wrong. And maybe the authorities did, too. If I had stood trial…if I had been judged and absolved by my peers…then maybe I could be free of this nightmare."

"There's something to that," Curran said. "So you won't be objecting to bringing in the authorities now. Here."

"No!"

His visage darkened. "Jane, you are not taking this seriously enough. Tonight, at best, someone was playing a deadly game with you. You could have been shot and killed."

"But I wasn't. And what if I was mistaken?"

"Let the authorities investigate."

"I can't do it, Curran, not yet," she insisted. "Bringing in the authorities too soon might warn off the guilty one."

"Good, then you'll be safe."

"Not good! I need to know for sure." She needed the truth about why Gavin duped her. "Besides, I wasn't really hurt. Not this time."

"Next time you could be dead. You need the right people on your side," Curran continued. "People— police—who know you and care about you."

"But the local police won't take me seriously, not without some kind of proof. After all, everyone knows I came back to Grantham Acres not quite right… And then word will get around and everyone will know what a fool I was. Please, Curran.'' Jane took another sip from her cup, but the tea had grown cold and bitter. "When I lay in that ravine, I wondered who could possibly want me dead, and why Gavin wanted Finn dead in the first place. What would he have gained? He wasn't a cruel man. I would swear his violence that night was against his nature.''

"I never found him to be cruel with his Thoroughbreds, either,'' Curran admitted.

"Then why?'' Jane asked, despair threatening to overwhelm her. "Could someone have forced him to it? Someone who believes I now know the whole truth when I really don't know anything? What if there *was* someone else involved?''

"A partner.''

"Or employer.''

Thoughtful, Curran said, "It won't be difficult to find out what owners Shaw worked for in the past year. I'll get Ned on it in the morning.''

"Why would another owner want to set me up?'' Jane asked.

Again Curran took a moment before saying, "I don't have all the answers, but if you're determined to be fighting me over bringing in the local authorities, then, all right, we'll figure it out together.''

That sounded good, but could she believe in him, especially when he had such power over her?

Gripping the arms of her chair, she demanded, "Tell me what you did to me out in the back acres.'' When Curran didn't immediately answer, she said, "I gave *you* what you wanted to know.''

Well, almost all of it, she silently added.

Curran nodded. "What is it you sensed?"

Immediately the images and emotions flowed through her again, the memory dreamlike.

A pasture…flowers…his holding her hand and them running…her knee healed and spirit soaring…

"A sense of calmness. Freedom. I could move normally. Think normally. With you." Dreamlike *now,* but what if it turned into another nightmare. "What have you done to me, Curran? What magic do you keep using on me?"

"Not magic," he insisted. "I told you about the connection."

"You put those thoughts in my head."

"I was merely trying to calm you. To give you an inner peace."

"Peace? You think I can have peace of mind when someone can get inside my head and screw around with it?"

"That's not what I did."

"Semantics, Curran, semantics. How far does this go?" she asked. She pushed herself out of her chair and stared down at him. "Where do you stop?"

"I don't know." Slowly, Curran rose to face her more directly. "As I told you before, I've not had a connection with any other human being."

Despite being so frightened by the experience that she couldn't control, Jane responded physically to Curran's closeness and the warmth of his breath across her face. Her pulse triggered and her mouth went dry.

"So I don't know where we can take this," he continued softly, his tone seductive.

He trailed a finger along the side of her face and she sucked in her breath. He would kiss her again, and here she was, dressed only in his robe. Thinking about that, she shuddered. Her body came alive, wanting more than a comforting embrace.

He whispered, "You're special—"

Those words a dash of cold water, she cried, "Stop!"

You're special, Jane.

Gavin had told her the same thing. Suddenly, she had the awful sensation of history repeating itself.

"I—I mean, don't do it again!" She backed off and crossed her arms in front of her so that he couldn't get any closer. "Get in my mind, I mean."

To her frustration, Curran said, "I can't promise any such thing. The connection between us has a life of its own. What I can promise is that you can trust me, Sheena."

A thrill shot through her at the use of the nickname. Jane *wanted* to trust Curran McKenna, but could she? She had put her trust in Gavin Shaw, another Irish horse trainer, and had almost died for her folly.

How could she be certain that Curran wouldn't give her equal reason for regret?

MORE THAN AN HOUR LATER, Jane left the guest house, refusing Curran's offer to escort her to her door. She needed time alone from him. Time to think.

Thankfully, Curran had backed down and given her some quiet time during which she had felt her equilibrium restored. Then they had talked about Finn—not about the violence done to him, but about his progress.

Jane entered the house. The downstairs was dark

and quiet. Nani must have retired for the evening, which meant no questions. At least not tonight. No doubt her grandmother suspected that something weird was going on. Curran was undoubtedly right when he'd suggested that Nani deserved to know the truth.

Just not tonight. She couldn't take any more truths tonight, Jane thought.

She took the stairs as quickly as she could, considering how badly her bruised body was beginning to hurt. Clean as she was, getting in her Jacuzzi to soak and vibrate out the aches and pains was sounding like a fine idea even at this late hour.

She was never so glad to get inside her own quarters.

When she turned on a low lamp that softly illuminated the jewel-blue walls, however, Jane realized she wasn't alone. Curled up in a wingback chair near the canopied mahogany bed, Susan blinked against the light as if she'd been asleep.

Immediately concerned, for this was not like her sister, Jane asked, "Susan, are you all right?"

"No, I'm not all right." The teenager untangled her limbs and easily got to her feet. "I'm totally humiliated. All because of *you*, Jane. I don't believe you went to Tim and spoke to him about me."

Wondering who had contacted whom, Jane calmly said, "He was using you, Susan."

"You don't know that."

"As a matter of fact, I do. He's assistant to Holt Easterling, who works for—"

"I know who he works for. So what?" Susan's voice went up a notch. "Everyone in this area has some connection to Thoroughbreds and people still manage to see each other, don't they?''

''I—I guess.''

''So Tim works for people who have a horse that is the favorite to win the Classic Cup. The one you bought won't even let a jockey on his back. So sure, I guess it makes a lot of sense that they'd get Tim to show interest in me so that he could spy on us to plan strategy.''

Put like that, it did seem a bit ridiculous, Jane admitted. Still, why else would a man Timothy Brady's age want to date a teenager?

Thinking about her grandmother's concern for her relationship with her sister, not to mention her own feelings, Jane decided she'd best try to smooth things over.

''Susan, I actually ran into Tim by chance this morning. I'm not certain that he told you this, but I already knew him from New York.''

''What?''

''He's the one who helped me out in Hudson Valley after the accident. I actually like the guy, but I still think the age difference…'' She stopped before she repeated herself and put her sister off further. ''I didn't set out to humiliate you, Susan, and I'm sorry if I did.''

''Sorry? According to you, I don't do anything right. And you want me to go live with Mother!''

Jane grimaced. ''I don't. I would miss you. I lost my temper before. I *am* sorry,'' she repeated.

''Really?''

''Truly. Grantham Acres is your home for as long as you want it to be. Or at least for as long as we still own it.''

''Oh, Jane,'' Susan said, launching herself at her sister. ''I'm sorry, too.''

Jane winced but kept herself from indicating that she was in pain. She hugged Susan and kissed the top of her head.

''I know the pressure you've been under trying to keep our home for us,'' Susan said. ''We won't really lose the farm, will we, Jane? It would kill Nani.''

It would kill her inside, too, Jane thought. What was left of her. She squeezed her sister tight.

''We have to stick together, kiddo. And we're not going to lose Grantham Acres if I can help it. We just have to pray that Curran can ready Finn for the race. If that's possible, I know Finn will run for us with his heart.''

Which was about all you could ask from another, whether a horse or a man.

HAVING PROMISED to find Jane's cane before Belle noticed that it was missing, Curran went after it straightaway with the first rays of dawn.

But that wasn't all he was looking for on the back acres. Starting where the cars had been parked, Curran carefully made his way into the stand of trees, his gaze sweeping the ground around him.

All he spotted, though, was the occasional footprint in the soft earth beneath the trees. Jane's. His. And that belonging to another man who wore a smaller shoe than his own.

Hunkering down to examine one of the prints more closely, he guessed it might have been made by a brogan. Not much he could tell from that except whoever had been out here wore a sensible work boot.

Curran rose and gazed around the area. Something that didn't belong at the edge of the clearing caught his eye.

A moment later, he was there, looking down at a tranquilizer dart.

What in the world…?

And then it hit him. Someone had been shooting at Jane, certainly, but not with bullets. Even so, a tranquilizer dart prepared to calm a large animal could wreak havoc on, if not kill, a human being.

Whoever had been after Jane, then, was an amateur rather than some professional hit man. Undoubtedly someone who worked with Thoroughbreds for a living, if the choice of weapon were any indication. The person hadn't even been clever enough to destroy the evidence. Or perhaps an amateur wouldn't even think that far ahead.

Taking a piece of paper from his pocket, he lifted the dart so as not to smear any fingerprints, if, indeed, there were any to be found. Just in case…

Curran put the dart in his pocket and went on, all the while thinking of the trouble Jane was in.

How could he save her when she seemed determined to hurl herself headlong into danger?

The local police were their best bet, but he had little hope of convincing her to do the smart thing. She was willing to make herself a target, all to learn the truth.

Why? What truth?

What more was there to her story than she had shared?

If only he had touched her…

Connecting with her for a second time that night would have been a wrong move, and Curran had known it. She had been freaked out about what had happened between them in the back acres and didn't want him inside her head.

Then, again, who would?

Even so, he thought, Jane was coming around, coming *to him,* but his trying to psych her out at the wrong moment would send her running the other way, the very thing that would destroy the possibilities between them. So he had to take extra care with her. He was beginning to realize that he wanted Jane right where she'd thrown herself when he'd found her on the ridge—in his arms.

Curran knew he could easily be one with his Sheena, could become part of her very soul.

A scary, scary thought.

Although he hadn't had the connection with Maggie Butler, he'd been madly in love with the beautiful widow and now he was falling for Jane. Not that it was the same thing. He wasn't the same unknown trainer without a punt in his pocket. And Jane was no Maggie—she was so very much more. Their working relationship was different, as well, but there it was—Jane was still his employer.

And he had a sneaking suspicion that the part of the story she hadn't told him would sound all too familiar.

Jane Grantham and Gavin Shaw.

Together?

Was that what her fear of exposure was all about? That everyone would know that she had taken someone below her blue-blooded stature as a lover?

Jane and Shaw—secret lovers—why hadn't it occurred to him until this very moment?

Having retraced his tracks to where he'd found

Jane, he grimly looked beyond, to the ravine where she'd fallen. His gut clenched. The incline looked so much more forbidding in the light of morning. She could have broken something in a fall like that, even her neck.

He spotted the cane almost immediately. It lay tangled in some underbrush halfway down the incline.

Curran took a step and his foot slid. He caught himself and proceeded with more care.

It took him several minutes to get down to the cane, and even longer to climb back up. He was in the best of physical condition and he fought the incline for safe footholds. He could only imagine how difficult the climb must have been for Jane, and in the dark.

But she was a woman without fear, at least when it came to the physical dangers in life.

As his head resurfaced over the ridge, his gaze lit on a bright bit of wrapper on the ground. He might have ignored it, but the footprint next to it made that impossible.

This was the very spot where the man had stood the night before, assuming that Jane was dead.

The hair on the back of his neck prickled, making him snatch up the discarded piece of foil. He started when he saw that it was candy wrapper, a product of Ireland.

Either Connemara Mints were a recent import or...

How many Irishman were in the area at the moment? Curran wondered. Besides himself and Ned, only one other person came to mind.

Timothy Brady.

Chapter Ten

When Curran drove up in front of the guest house, Ned was coming out. Wondering what his assistant had been up to, Curran met him at the porch steps.

"I was just looking for you," Ned explained. "Out and around so early?"

He raised his bushy eyebrows as if awaiting an explanation. Curran wasn't about to share more than necessary with anyone yet. He had given Jane his word, after all.

"Ned, I need you to make some calls for me. You remember Gavin Shaw, don't you?"

His assistant hesitated a second before echoing, "Shaw. Yes, of course."

"I'm trying to get some information on the man, which means tracking down his associates over the past year."

"What kind of information?"

"It's personal," Curran said. "You merely get names and numbers of the owners he worked for, and I'll do the rest."

"Yes, sir," Ned groused.

Moving back toward his own quarters, Ned seemed disgruntled at the task. Curran could hardly blame him. He was an assistant horse trainer without a horse.

Hopefully, that was about to change.

Curran went inside and wolfed down a big breakfast, after which he proceeded to the barn. Jimi was already dressed and waiting for him.

"No Jane?" Curran asked.

"Haven't seen her this morning."

He'd thought he'd handled things well the night before. Perhaps not as well as he had hoped.

He kept watch for her as he rounded up Finn himself—no problem there anymore—and invited Jimi inside the paddock to walk with them.

"So what do you think?" the jockey asked, his young face eager as he paced alongside Curran, Finn following so as to be part of the "herd." "Do I get a shot to ride him today, or what?"

"We'll see how things progress," Curran said, a bit distracted at wondering why Jane hadn't yet shown. "But yes, I do believe you have a shot."

When he brought out the lunge line and tried attaching it to Finn's halter, however, Curran had another think coming. Finn threw up his head and, with eyes rolling wildly, backed off, the stallion's fear no doubt directly related to his being tied up and helpless. Curran wasn't really surprised that he had more work to do. Each item that jogged the horse's memory could present a new threat.

"I think you had best get out of the way for now, lad," Curran said, pointing to the fence.

Sighing, Jimi followed instructions and was soon perched on the top fence rail. He watched as Curran began pacing around the paddock. Each time Finn closed in, Curran flicked the line out. At first wary and skittish, the stallion eventually got used to seeing the line snake out at him without hurting him and merely hesitated until Curran pulled it back in.

"He's one troubled horse," Jimi said. "But he likes you and wants your approval."

"Your turn next."

"You want me to get in there and torture him like that? I don't know that he likes me too much. He might eat me like a snack."

"If you're afraid of him, you'll never be able to ride him," Curran said. "Animals sense fear more acutely than human beings do."

"Nah, I ain't afraid!"

"Then you'll have to prove it."

Curran hung the lunge line on the fence and approached Finn directly. When the horse eyed him warily, he walked right by him and circled toward the barn. Hearing hooves hit the dirt behind him, Curran grinned. At least he hadn't lost all the ground he had gained.

Not with the horse, anyway.

But considering Jane hadn't yet shown her face, he wasn't so certain about her.

JANE WAS ON HER WAY OUT of the house, her destination the barn, when Curran came face-to-face with her as she stepped off the stoop.

"Your cane," he said, his voice friendlier than his expression.

"Thank you." She took it from him. "I really appreciate this."

"Too busy to be joining us this morning?"

"Actually, yes." Nerves still taut, she fiddled with the silver horse head. "Unfortunately, Nani and I were having a heated discussion and I couldn't exactly leave in the middle of things."

"You told her?"

"You convinced me that she had a right to know," Jane admitted. "Who can say what will happen next. Nani doesn't miss a thing, and another set of eyes won't be amiss."

"Or several sets, some official."

"No police."

Although she'd had to argue that point with Nani even more strenuously than she had with Curran. To be truthful, Jane wasn't certain that her grandmother would hold off calling her old friend, Sheriff Biggs Mason.

"I found more than your cane this morning," Curran said, pulling a small object from his pocket.

Taking the plastic zipped bag holding a single item from him, Jane frowned. "What in the world was a tranquilizer dart doing out there?"

"The man who was trying to kill you wasn't using bullets," Curran said simply.

"Then maybe he didn't mean to kill me, after all."

"You think not?"

If the dart could bring down a large animal...

"You're right, of course," Jane said, suddenly feeling queasy and handing the potential weapon back to him. "Tranquilized to death. Who would have thought?"

"Someone who works with horses. Not a professional killer. Not even a talented amateur."

"I don't get it. What are you trying to tell me?"

"That this man does sloppy work. And he's reckless."

"Then maybe we'll get lucky."

"Or maybe he'll get even more careless. I'm sure this is something you haven't been thinking on too closely," Curran said, "but what if the danger isn't just to you?"

"Finn will be fine. We have the new security code on the barn and Jimi is determined to sleep outside his stall every night."

"I wasn't meaning Finn. What about your grandmother? Your sister?"

A frisson of fear washed through her. "They don't know anything. No one has any quarrel with them."

"But what if they get in the way?"

Something that hadn't occurred to her. Jane wrestled with the sick feeling that suddenly filled her.

What to do?

"I would try sending them away for their own good if I thought I had a snowball's chance in hell of making it happen. Nani would outright refuse. The farm is her home, and no one is going to put her out, at least not while the Granthams still own the place. As for Susan..." Jane knew her sister would see being sent away as a betrayal, especially after their heart-to-heart of the night before. But which was more important, her sister's feelings or her safety? "I suppose I could insist Susan go to Mother for her own protection."

"I don't believe you!"

"Susan!" Jane whipped around and saw her sister standing in the doorway. "I didn't know you were there."

"Obviously not." Susan's face was nearly as red as the shirt she wore. "Liar!"

"You don't understand. I can explain."

But did she want to?

Not that the teenager waited for any justification. With a sob, she fled past them to her car.

"Susan!" Jane called, to no avail.

Only seconds later, the car was down the driveway.

"I'm going to have to tell her," Jane said, stunned. "It's the only way. What made me think I could keep my dignity?"

Curran put an arm around her shoulders. "Susan won't think any less of you for the truth. She's your blood. She will understand."

His touch was comforting. Somehow, he managed to make her feel as if everything would be all right in the end.

"You really think so?" she asked.

"Aye."

Jane ached to throw herself at Curran again so that she could feel his arms around her. But that wouldn't be wise. She knew what could happen if they touched. Then a rough cough made her pull away instead and she saw Ned Flaherty a few yards off.

"I'll be begging your pardon, but I have that information you wanted."

"Ned, what did you find out?" Curran asked.

"Last summer, Gavin Shaw trained a few horses for Paddy O'Connor and one for Liam Black, but no one knows what he's been up to since."

That Curran was asking around about Gavin astonished Jane, since he hadn't said a thing about it to her. She didn't know whether or not to be upset. Curran was, after all, merely trying to get to the truth to protect her.

"I can certainly give Liam and Paddy a call, though those connections may have been too long

ago to be of use to us now. Shaw was at the Keeneland meet here in Kentucky last October,'' Curran
told Ned. ''So he must have been working for someone, possibly an American.'' He glanced at Jane.
''You wouldn't know who that might be?''

She shook her head. ''I only met Gavin then, remember. If he ever mentioned a name, I don't remember. But it won't be hard to find out.''

''What kind of information are you wanting?''
Ned asked.

''I don't know,'' Curran and Jane answered in unison.

''If this has something to do with Finn mac Cumhail, I should be informed,'' Ned said, looking point-
edly at Curran. ''Shaw didn't work with him, did
he?''

Jane frowned at Curran, who then said, ''Not exactly.''

When his employer wasn't more forthcoming, a
flare of displeasure quickly crossed the assistant
trainer's features before disappearing beneath his
customary smile.

Jane wondered about Ned's reaction for a moment,
but then figured the man had to be frustrated. Curran
was asking for his help without telling him everything. For which she was quite thankful. The fewer
people who knew what a fool she had been, the better.

Although in the end, she mused, it would undoubtedly all come out in the wash.

''We can go over to the library at the Keeneland
track,'' she suggested. ''Last year, the *Daily Racing
Form* donated their complete archive of newspapers
and other publications to the library.''

The owner and trainer of each horse that raced being listed, they would easily find the name of Gavin's employer, especially since the Keeneland meet only lasted for three weeks.

"Later," Curran agreed. "I don't want to let down on Finn now that we have him."

"We do?" Ned asked.

"In a manner of speaking. We have a ways to go. But it's time for you to introduce yourself to the lad."

"Let's be about it, then."

Her mind on things more important than Finn's progress, Jane followed, her determination to find answers as to Gavin Shaw's perfidy stronger than ever.

THE BARONIAL LIBRARY at Keeneland gave them what they needed—the name of Gavin's employer at the fall meet.

"Dennis Becke," Jane said. "I don't know him personally, but I know of him. In the past, Daddy sold him a few of our colts and mares. I'm certain that he has horses stabled at Churchill Downs."

"There is racing today." Curran checked his watch. "If he had any entries, we should still be able to catch him."

They quickly scanned the current *Daily Racing Form* to confirm the fact that, indeed, three of Becke's horses had been scheduled to race.

Leaving the library, whose gray stone facade was covered by a network of ivy, they crossed the grounds that had been fashioned into a parklike setting with myriad trees, including dogwoods, sycamores and maples. Jane had always thought the Keeneland architecture and landscaping to be stately, more like an East Coast university than a racetrack. More trees framed a panoramic view of the surrounding bluegrass countryside—tobacco barns amidst bands of grazing horses—a site that never failed to stir Jane's love of her home state. Even the parking lot was lined with pin oaks.

More familiar with the roads, she opted to drive.

They were on the pike headed toward Louisville before she said, "I assume you have a plan when we find Becke. I wouldn't know where to start."

"I'm hoping he'll tell us something about Shaw's associates. Maybe a name will ring a bell for you. Someone who can suggest what he was into, why he would have been willing to break Finn's legs."

He didn't add *why he'd been willing to kill her*.

What knowing would get her was as elusive as the information itself. It wouldn't make her feel better. Wouldn't give back her trust in human nature.

But Jane was certain she needed to know or she and Finn and Grantham Acres were all doomed.

The drive took less than an hour. They arrived at Churchill Downs, as different from Keeneland as could be. Rather than a rural location, this was the in the heart of the city. The building was blinding white and distinguished by its famous twin spires.

They arrived just before the last race began. People were already heading out in droves. As they walked against the crowd, Jane was jammed by an obviously disgruntled bettor—a loser, no doubt—and Curran put a protective arm around her shoulders to steady her.

Her pulse kicked up as it always seemed to when he touched her, no matter how innocently, but she put her mind to their purpose. Becke's last horse had already run.

Fearing they might be too late to catch him, she immediately headed for the backstretch. Curran hung on to her, steadying her even while pushing her to move faster. Horses for the last race were already in the paddock. At the backstretch security gates, they showed the guards their identification that labeled them as horse people and got directions to Becke's barn.

Despite the late hour, the area was busy. They passed hotwalkers cooling down horses from a previous race, grooms who were bathing their charges before stabling them for the night and a couple of jockeys who were arguing about an unsuccessful ride.

By the time they reached the right barn, Jane felt as if she'd run a marathon. But the rush had paid off. They caught Dennis Becke just as he was waving goodbye to his crew. Jane recognized his silver hair and distinctive sunglasses instantly as they approached him beneath the underhang.

"Mr. Becke, may we have a few minutes of your time?" she asked, looking up at the man who was taller than Curran. "I'm Jane Grantham of Grantham Acres, and this is Curran McKenna—"

"I knew your father," Becke interrupted, shaking Jane's hand. And then he pumped Curran's. "And I certainly know who you are. I saw Sligo Red win the Irish Champion Stakes at Leopardstown. If you're here looking for work, I'm interested in talking to you. I was thinking of buying some new horses anyway and I hear you have the touch."

"Ah, now there's some blarney," Curran said with

a laugh. "I appreciate the compliment, but actually, I'm wanting to talk to you about Gavin Shaw."

"Shaw." Becke's smile faded a tad. "What has he gotten himself into?"

"That's what we're trying to find out," Jane hedged, wondering if Becke was aware that Gavin had dropped out of sight.

But Jane knew he hadn't a clue when he said, "I don't know how I can help you since I haven't seen him since last November." Which had been shortly after she'd met him.

Curran said, "How is it that Shaw worked for you?"

"He came over with a couple of Irish Thoroughbreds I had just bought. It was to be a temporary situation. Get them settled in and all."

"And were you satisfied with him?"

"Yes, of course. He had a nice rapport with the animals."

"He never did anything…cruel to any of your horses, did he?" Jane asked.

"What? No, of course not! Actually, when I saw how well the horses responded to him, I asked him to stay. I gave him a few of my older mounts who hadn't been doing so well, also. I wanted to see if he could do better with them than my current trainer. And it seemed as if he would have."

"But he didn't stay," Jane said.

"Not nearly long enough." Becke shook his head. "He had some personal problems—I knew that right away—but what man in this crazy business doesn't."

Curran and Jane exchanged looks.

"What kind of problems?" Curran asked.

"He liked the high life. Drinking, women, betting. The usual."

The usual.

Jane cringed inside. Obviously she hadn't been the only woman Gavin had wooed. Though perhaps she'd been the only one so naive, so trusting...

Would she ever be able to trust a man again? she wondered, glancing sideways at Curran.

Becke went on, "Shaw's pursuits were fairly harmless, I thought, until suddenly he grew very morose. There were a few odd phone calls and then without giving me notice, he up and returned to Ireland."

"Have you any idea why?" Curran asked.

"Pressing business, he said. Something he couldn't get out of...or some debt he owed someone. I'm not quite clear on the details. And I'm sorry that I can't tell you more."

"Maybe someone else can. His friends, perhaps?"

"He hung around with a couple of other Irishmen. An owner named Ian McCurdy—he's now based at Santa Anita. And Sean Harris, a local sportswriter. Actually, he writes for the *Lexington Record*." Becke paused for only a second. "How much trouble is Shaw in?"

"Too much. We thank you for your assistance."

Curran was the one hedging this time, Jane thought, wondering if Dennis Becke was going to challenge him for details.

But the owner merely gave him a considering look before saying, "No problem. And if you do decide to settle here in Kentucky, keep me in mind. I'm always looking for a top-notch trainer."

Dennis Becke headed out, as he had intended before their arrival. Jane glanced at a nearby blood bay who gazed at her curiously from his stall as he munched on a mouthful of hay. Unable to resist, she stroked his velvet nose. He lipped her hand as if looking for a treat and snorted in disgust when he didn't find it.

Jane grinned despite their serious mission.

"Let's find a house phone," Curran said, "and call up to the press box to see if Sean Harris is still around."

"We can try, but the last race just ended," Jane said, indicating the horses being led back to their stalls. Then she spotted a phone at the end of the shed row. "Over there, Curran."

As they made their way toward it, he said, "So we were right about Shaw's actions being out of step."

"He must have been terribly desperate."

Jane thought again of Gavin's intensity as he slashed with the pipe first at Finn, then at her. What could have caused such uncharacteristic behavior?

And what dark forces were still at work against her?

Curran's call up to the press box took only a minute. Harris had already left.

"It seems as if we're on a wild-goose chase," Jane said.

"I shall catch up to Harris later."

"Or Timothy Brady," Jane suggested. "I didn't even think to find out what he might know about Gavin's troubles, and he was Gavin's assistant."

"'Tis worth a try," Curran agreed. "And he might be on the grounds."

They got directions from one of the hotwalkers to

the barn where Stonehenge was stabled and immediately set off to see if they could find Tim. As they drew closer to Mukhtar Saladin's barn, a raised woman's voice echoed from within.

"You assured me that you could handle this!"

Jane heard a low male response, but she couldn't identify the speaker or make out what the man was saying.

"Too much is riding on this—keep that in mind."

Suddenly, Phyllis rounded the building alone, and upon seeing Curran and Jane, stood stock-still, her frozen expression one of unpleasant surprise.

But only for a moment.

"Jane, darling...and Curran!" Quickly thawing, the society matron advanced on them, a smile pulling at her mouth, her arms spread wide in welcome. "What brings you two here today?"

A movement from the shed row caught Jane's attention. A man pulling back into the shadows. Unless she was imagining things, he was purposely avoiding them.

"We would be getting the lay of the land for next week," Curran said, turning Jane's attention back to their unexpected encounter.

Phyllis's smile faltered once more. "You mean that Finn mac Cumhail will be ready for the Classic?"

"Curran is something of a tease," Jane said, avoiding a straight answer. Truth be told, she still wasn't certain that the stallion would come through for them so quickly. "Actually, we're here looking for Timothy Brady."

Phyllis stared at her, expression blank as if she

didn't know who Tim was. And perhaps not. Perhaps an assistant trainer was beneath her notice.

But before Jane could clarify, Mukhtar Saladin himself appeared and Phyllis's demeanor changed instantly, a frisson of something dark—fear?—crossing her neutral expression. Saladin himself seemed displeased.

Tension oozed from them both.

"My little raven," Saladin said, his voice low but firm. "We need to finish that discussion." He glanced at Jane and Curran, and then summarily dismissed them. "In private."

Had Phyllis been arguing with Saladin? Jane had the feeling not. Whoever the woman had been berating hadn't wanted to face them, and Jane doubted Phyllis would so much as speak an ill word to her newest beau.

Confirming that conclusion, Phyllis purred, "Yes, darling, of course," and gave Saladin a look of adoration. "Now, if the two of you will excuse us—"

"Wait!" Jane said. "What about Timothy Brady?"

Saladin glowered at her. "If Brady is here, then he is working with one of my horses. I do not want his time taken up with idle chatter."

Wrapping an arm around Phyllis's shoulders, he swept her away for that privacy he'd demanded.

Leaving Jane wondering if Tim had been the source of the earlier altercation—Phyllis probably wouldn't have had any compunction against speaking harshly to a trainer or especially to an assistant. Now Phyllis was doing her best to appease an angry Saladin.

There was trouble brewing in paradise...if not trouble of a more serious nature.

JANE GRANTHAM WASN'T DEAD. That fact nearly choked him.

What the hell had gone wrong? He'd seen her lying there, at the bottom of the ravine, all the life drained out of her.

Or so he had thought.

Too many assumptions. He must have missed her completely, and she had merely fallen.

Why hadn't he double-checked?

He couldn't take his eyes off her and McKenna as they walked through the backstretch, so eager to find the truth.

Well, the truth was going to find them. Both of them. And they weren't going to like it.

Damn!

How could things keep going from bad to worse? he wondered. He'd known McKenna was going to be trouble, but what he hadn't realized was that he might be forced to kill more than a defenseless woman.

Chapter Eleven

On the way home to Grantham Acres, Jane suggested they stop for a meal at a cozy, brick-faced restaurant just off the highway. Suspecting that she wanted to avoid a dinner confrontation with Susan, Curran readily agreed.

They could use a little downtime, an hour just for the two of them, away from the farm's financial troubles and the search for the identity of a potential murderer. Truth be told, he simply wanted to be with her.

And being so close, he naturally wanted to touch her, but after her last warning about not getting into her mind, he figured discretion was in order. It took great restraint for him not to wrap his arm around Jane's waist as they went from car to building. The Black Stallion was obviously named after the owner's prized Thoroughbred. They passed photos of the magnificent horse lining the walls from the foyer into the cozy dining room.

Seated in a dark corner and with their orders taken, a full pint before him, Curran started to relax.

And then Jane mused, "What could Phyllis Singleton-Volmer be trying to hide?"

Not exactly the dinner conversation he'd anticipated, Curran thought, taking a swig of his beer.
"What makes you think she's hiding anything?"

"Her reaction when she saw us. That was certainly
some double take."

The socialite had seemed a bit taken aback, Curran
remembered, but then she'd been arguing with someone and undoubtedly had been in a dark mood. Only
with whom had she been at odds? he wondered.
Other than Saladin himself.

He said, "It seems to me that she merely put on
a good face so no one has anything to criticize."

"Not everything is about appearances."

"Could have fooled me."

"Now why do I get the feeling that barb is meant
for me?" Jane asked, her complexion flushing with
soft color.

Wanting to kiss her, Curran restrained himself.
"Feeling guilty?"

"Sometimes."

The way she said it made him think that Jane had
just moved into a whole different territory. Giving
up on the thought that she might just want to spend
a few moments alone with him, he put his own de-
sires aside for the moment.

"You feel guilty about Shaw?" he asked.

"I have enough reason."

Fighting his better judgment, Curran reached
across the table and took Jane's hand to comfort her.
She jumped as if stung. He clung to her fingers and
refused to let her withdraw. For a moment, they
merely shared the warmth of two human beings connecting on a very basic level.

Then suddenly, as if an invisible force took on a

life of its own, the connection between them multiplied and metamorphosed...

He felt her fear, her desperation... He experienced the weight of the pitchfork in her hands.

Horror filled him when Shaw bolted forward and impaled himself on the tines. He staggered back and somehow wrested himself free of the implement. Blood gushed through his fingers as he tried to stop it.

Curran watched, mesmerized, shaking...

But it was Jane who was shaking, and in reliving her memory he was somehow inside her.

He pushed back at the dreadful images and emotions, crowded them with projected security and warmth that he wanted to give her...

Across from him, Jane's eyes widened.

Message received, Curran thought as he blinked back into reality.

"Stop that!" Jane whispered, trying to free her hand. "I told you not to do that anymore!"

Still, Curran wouldn't let her go. "Shaw meant you harm, Jane. You were merely protecting yourself. And now I want to protect you."

Her expression changed—to one of longing?—but only for a moment. Then she shook away whatever she was feeling. And with a show of strength, she plucked her hand from his.

So that he couldn't read her further?

"I can't rationalize this!" she insisted. "If only..."

"If only what?"

"Never mind." She cast her eyes downward. "Nothing."

"I'm on your side."

"Are you?"

"Whose side would I be on, then?"

She glanced up at him. "Your own."

Curran was certain that she hadn't come to that conclusion naturally. He was certain that she had been done harm in more ways than she had yet admitted.

"At least you're honest about your opinion of me. Life must have treated you terribly for you to be so cynical," he said, in truth thinking of Gavin Shaw.

"Only lately. I'm afraid the past few months have colored my view of the world." Her breath trembled as she said, "I used to be a trusting person."

He remembered a time when he had been trusting, as well. "We all start out that way."

"Even you?" She looked up at him through wounded eyes.

Softening to her hurt, he admitted, "Even me."

Dinner arrived, cutting the heart-to-heart to the quick. They ate in silence. Ate fast. The hour that Curran had anticipated dwindled to half.

And through it all, Curran felt her gaze on him, as if she was trying to see inside him.

What a turnaround that would be...

Only when the coffee arrived did she ask, "What about you, Curran? I feel as if you know everything about me, but I know nothing about you...other than your being Irish, a talented horse trainer, and a man with two sisters and a gift that he doesn't particularly appreciate."

And one that she didn't altogether appreciate, either, he knew. "What more do you need?"

She shrugged. "The usual. What kind of a child

were you? What was your most heartfelt dream? Have you ever had your heart broken?''

"Somewhat inventive…I'm doing it…and yes.''

"Well, no waste of words there.''

She hadn't confided in him totally about Shaw, so why should he tell her about Maggie?

"What you see is what you get.''

"I think I said that,'' she protested.

"That you did.'' Curran moved a seat closer so that he was next to rather than across from her. The golden brown hair feathering her face gave her that earthly quality he loved about her. He stared into her sparkling eyes and was once again drawn in. "I *like* what I see—a woman who is strong and protective of those she loves, plus has a tender heart.''

She licked her lips. "Who is unsure of herself, foolish and has a slightly tarnished outlook on life.''

"That's the problem. How is it that you can only see the negative about yourself?''

"Experience.''

Curran cupped her chin and turned her lovely face toward him. "Let me give you a new one, then.''

He could feel the pulse in her throat speed up against the part of his hand touching it. Her breath quickened and her eyes widened as he slowly dipped his head toward hers.

His own breath caught as his mouth grazed hers. Her lips trembled and began to open for him. His pulse surged with expectation…

Then suddenly she pulled back, her expression strange. "No!''

"You want me to kiss you, Sheena,'' he said in a low, seductive voice. "I don't need to have special powers to know that.''

"But not here." She furtively glanced around as if worried someone was watching. "Not like this."

"I see."

She slid her glance away and settled herself in her chair away from him as far as she could without actually getting up and moving.

That was it, then, Curran thought, removing himself and settling back in his original seat. In the secretive dark, with no one to see, kissing him might be acceptable to the farm owner. But in the open...

"You're a snob, then, Jane Grantham," he said, comparing her to Maggie and finding no difference where it counted. "A lowly horse trainer is not good enough for the likes of you."

He hadn't actually meant to say it aloud, but the words left his mouth without permission. Curran had had enough of shaming her kind. He wouldn't take them back.

And though Jane turned a stricken gaze on him, she didn't make any denials.

LET HIM THINK what he would, Jane wasn't about to unburden herself to Curran McKenna.

She *had* wanted him to kiss her again, but she hadn't let him because the memories of Gavin were too raw after reliving the horror of his death.

And because it would have given Curran permission to get inside her head and go exploring yet again. He did that more than enough for her comfort and she couldn't seem to stop him. Surely even she was entitled to some privacy of thought.

To that end, she just had to avoid getting too close, no matter how tempting a Curran McKenna might be.

Not that he was one of many. Curran was unique. Perhaps special.

The one.

But how could she be sure? Jane wondered. He put her emotions in turmoil, but how could she trust her own instincts after the way she'd led her family and farm and a horse who couldn't protect himself into ruin?

She couldn't do that again and survive.

The return drive seemed interminable and Jane was relieved when they arrived at Grantham Acres. Dusk had fallen, masking Curran's expression when she glanced at him. He stopped the car in front of the house.

Slipping out, she said, "I'll see you in the morning."

Maybe a night alone to think things through would help her sort out all her doubts.

"In the morning, then," he repeated coolly.

A shiver went up her spine and she stood planted to the spot, unable to make her limbs move as he drove off toward the guest house. His hurt cut her to the quick.

Surely he couldn't feel the knife as sharply as she...or could he?

Fearing she was being unfair to Curran in comparing him to Gavin in any way, Jane knew she had to deal with this situation. Deal with herself. *She* was the problem. She couldn't go on like this.

She couldn't expect him to.

Sighing, she turned toward the house and opened the door.

She'd barely set a foot inside when her grandmother called out, "Jane, dear, is that you?"

"Yes, Nani."

Her grandmother stepped into the foyer. One look at her distraught expression, and Jane knew something terrible had happened.

"Nani?"

"It's Susan."

Jane's pulse kicked up, as did a frisson of guilt. "What has she done now?"

"About an hour ago, she rushed out of here. Not a word to me about where she was going. Then a few minutes ago, I was on my way upstairs and I found this."

From her pocket, she pulled a piece of paper and handed it to Jane, who unfolded it and scanned the contents.

Printed in block letters, the missive was short.

S—
I MUST SEE YOU. MEET ME OUT AT THE POTTERS' FARM at 7:30.

T

"T-Timothy Brady," Jane murmured. "He didn't say where exactly." As far as she knew, in addition to the tobacco fields, there were a couple of barns and an abandoned house on the property. No one to see what they might be up to. She checked her watch. "It's just before eight now. Perhaps they'll still be at the barn. I'm going after her."

She opened the foyer-table drawer and took out the car keys.

"I'll go with you."

"No, Nani. This is my doing. You were right, I should have handled things with Susan better. She wouldn't have gone to meet Timothy Brady if she hadn't thought I was going to send her away.''

Which she still might do, but not until she'd explained why. She would tell her sister everything, Jane vowed, if only Susan were all right.

"Don't worry, Nani," she said, giving her grandmother a hug. "I'll bring Susan back safe and sound.''

"Of course you will, Jane. I can always count on you to do the right thing.''

If only that were true, Jane thought, setting off.

But this had to be true. Susan was her responsibility. She had to keep her little sister safe.

The note could be innocent, Jane assured herself as she started the car. Perhaps Timothy just wanted to say goodbye in person.

But he wasn't going to get away, she vowed, not without answering a few questions about Gavin. She realized that meant she would have to talk to him in front of Susan. Well, so be it. As Curran had said, she should have confided in her own blood long ago. She'd been foolish trying to protect them. Instead, she'd done just the opposite.

Whatever happened, confrontation with Tim or not, Jane vowed to explain things to Susan, so that her sister would understand the danger they were all in.

And then she would see to Curran, she thought. He had only done good by them. He had no investment here, really. He couldn't be certain that Finn would be ready for the Classic, no less win the cup. Yet here he was, giving her his all while she gave him a hard time.

This connection thing...while it scared her, she

couldn't ignore the significance of this happening only between the two of them. It had to mean something in the scheme of the universe.

She wanted to be able to trust in someone, Jane thought, not only with the farm, but with her heart.

And Curran McKenna seemed to be just the man to fit the bill.

CURRAN COULDN'T DEFINE what was troubling him.

More than the disquiet caused by the averted kiss, a strange unease filled him and wouldn't let him be.

"Sheena."

The name rolled from his lips so easily. She was his first thought when he awoke, his last thought at night. She filled the empty spaces in a way no woman ever had before.

Even as he thought about Jane Grantham being his fate, the telephone rang. Pulse speeding, he quickly snatched up the receiver.

"Jane?"

"I'm afraid not, Curran. 'Tis only your favorite sister."

"Flanna," he joked, "calling me all the way from Ireland, are you?"

"Be careful that I don't slap you silly," Keelin said with mock indignation. "I am still older than you."

Despite his mood, Curran smiled. He and his sisters had always tortured each other good-naturedly.

After exchanging pleasantries about family members, he asked, "So to what do I owe this pleasure?"

"I've been worried about you, boyo," she said bluntly. "So, tell me."

As usual, he needed no translation for the shorthand that came easily between them. "You need to hear me say that you were right?"

"So Jane Grantham is the one, then?"

"Aye, I'm afraid so. Not that she appreciates the fact."

"You told her?"

"Not exactly. Actually, 'tis me she doesn't appreciate. Rather, my being below her station." A fact that still stung.

Keelin was silent for a moment. "From what you've told me, she seemed more than that."

"I thought so, too."

"Perhaps you're reading her wrong," she suggested. "Perhaps 'tis something else that is making her unreceptive. Besides, she's an American and Americans are notoriously blind to class," she said, dismissing his objection. "Well, most of them, anyway."

"I would that you were right on this."

"What about the rest? The danger? I've not felt quiet about it since talking to you last."

"As you predicted," Curran admitted. "Someone tried to kill Jane using a tranquilizer dart."

"So it has started then."

Keelin's dire tone sent the short hairs on Curran's neck to attention. "And she won't let the authorities in on this, either."

"We McKennas don't pick mates who are easy to love."

"Sheena's easy enough to love, just difficult to get along with."

"Ah, so *she's* the difficult one."

Knowing Keelin was trying to lighten the mood, Curran said, "But not as difficult as you."

She laughed. "And what about the stallion? Have you tamed *him* yet?"

"He's coming along."

"I spoke to Tyler and he's agreed. Should Finn mac Cumhail be ready to run, we'll be there to see it—"

"I'll hold you to that, now."

"And to meet your Jane, of course."

Curran didn't protest that Jane wasn't his. He merely had to figure out how to convince her that she was.

Once they had signed off, Curran's unease returned twofold. Perhaps he was projecting, but he was certain that his disquiet had to do with Jane. But how, when they weren't in the same building, not to mention the same room?

As if he could connect with her anyway, Curran concentrated on what seemed to be an internal alarm that was going off, and had the singular feeling that Jane was definitely in danger.

Now!

JANE PULLED OFF the pike onto a dirt road that cut through the Potters' tobacco field and put on her brights. The road ahead was empty of life. But when she approached the twin wooden barns that were used to dry the crop, the high beams caught Susan's car, which was parked to the rear.

A bit wary, Jane looked around carefully as she drove closer, passing the system of flues coming from an exterior furnace that provided the curing heat.

No other vehicle in sight.

Had Tim not shown yet? Or had Susan gone with

him? To the abandoned house? Or farther away, perhaps for good?

Which was her greatest fear at the moment...

Jane closed her eyes and prayed that her first assumption—Tim not showing—was correct. Or, perhaps he had shown, had said his goodbyes and had left Susan to cope with her disappointment.

Whatever the circumstances, Jane needed to be sure.

Leaving the security of her car, she called out, "Susan?" but her sister didn't answer.

Jane grabbed her flashlight and cane and slipped into the night. Her gait awkward, she quickly cut through her car's high beams and went straight for her sister's vehicle. She flashed her portable light around the interior.

No one inside.

"Susan?" she called again, feeling a little sick inside as she scanned the area for something, anything, to lead her to the rash teenager.

Nothing.

Jane turned toward the barns used for flue-curing tobacco. They were high and narrow, each airtight building acting as a sort of chimney. No sign of life there, either. And a curing barn would be an odd place for a tryst, but she wouldn't know for certain unless she checked inside.

Susan's car was, after all, still here.

Opening the door of the first barn, she was immediately struck by the dry air. Regulated humidity and heat within the buildings dried the leaves so that they didn't become moldy and useless. Though she didn't condone smoking, tobacco was a major crop and a fact of life in the area, so she was familiar with the process.

She slipped inside and cast her flashlight beam across racks of tobacco leaves that were already turning yellow. The color would be fixed and all the moisture removed within a matter of days.

"Susan?" she called, moving inward, just to be sure she didn't miss anything.

Finding no sign of her sister, Jane left the first barn and headed for its twin. If Susan wasn't in there, she could check the house, but somehow, she didn't see Susan having a tryst in an abandoned building. She could be gone. A runaway.

Then what?

Susan was a minor. If she was missing, they would have to involve the authorities, after all. Nani could call Biggs Mason. The old sheriff had been a good friend for years. Surely he could be counted on to be efficient and discreet in bringing Susan home.

Bringing in the authorities should make Curran happy, Jane thought, wishing he were with her. In a very short time, she had grown dependent on his support and she ached to feel his arm around her shoulders, ached to hear the thrilling lilt of his voice.

"Curran, if you're tuning in to me, I do need you," she whispered.

And not just to fix her troubles.

When she swung open the door to the second building, she was blasted by dry air far hotter than in the first. This tobacco was obviously further along. The automatic rise in temperature was meant to dry the leaves thoroughly.

Nearly choking on the air—thankfully, no smoke or fumes were created in the flue-curing process—

she started an inspection that was cursory and quick until a spot of bright red flashed at her from between the dull yellow rows of tobacco.

Her sister had worn a red blouse that morning, Jane remembered.

"Susan?"

Leaning more heavily on her cane, she forced herself forward and was rewarded with a human sound. A moan? And then she spotted her.

"Susan!" she gasped.

Her sister lay on the floor, hands behind her back, duct tape sealing shut her mouth. Her face was nearly as red as her shirt and her skin looked basted. Her open eyes were filled with panic.

Heart pounding, Jane rushed forward. "Susan! Oh, Lord, did Tim do this to you?"

She dropped the cane and fell to her knees unthinking, then, stunned, froze in agony. Her sister's whimpers made her block out her own pain. When she took a steadying breath, immediately her mouth went dry.

Clamping her jaw shut tight against the dry heat, she set the flashlight down on the ground and gently began working the duct tape free so that the teenager could at least breathe better.

"Jane!" Susan gasped. "Get—"

"Don't try to talk!" Jane reached behind her sister to get at the bonds securing her wrists. "I'll have you out of here in a minute."

"No, get out!"

Susan's words were immediately followed by the sound of the barn door closing. Jane's pulse threaded unevenly. She pushed to her feet and moved as fast as she could, but what sounded like the door being jammed scraped up her spine.

In denial, she tried ripping at the handle, but the door wouldn't give. They were locked in, and the building was airtight.

What now? she wondered in shock.

The heat was already becoming intolerable. The whole flue-curing process could be accomplished in less than a week rather than the month it would take if the tobacco were air-dried. And the process was coming to a head.

The barn was going to get increasingly hotter.

Unless she could figure a way out, Jane realized, she and Susan would dehydrate just like the racks of yellowing tobacco leaves around them.

BACKING AWAY from the barn, he shuddered at his own handiwork. The sisters would both be found dead in the morning when the barns were opened and the tobacco inspected.

Dehydrated to death—a horrible way to go, but what wouldn't be?

He'd had to do it, he told himself. He'd had no choice. Too bad he'd had to involve the girl.

Now he had to remove any trace of their being here so that the night security guard wouldn't see anything amiss and feel the need to check inside.

He'd gone too far to let things go awry once again.

He shone his flashlight in Jane's vehicle. To his relief, she hadn't removed the keys. And he'd already gotten the other set off the sister.

He climbed inside and drove a short way farther down the road, away from the tobacco fields and toward the abandoned house. From what he could tell, no one came this way, at least not often. He left the car in a pocket of brush and jogged back to do the same with the girl's.

The really awful part was finished.

And he had no doubt that, when the bodies were found, no one would be thinking about the horse.

Chapter Twelve

Curran's nerves were fairly buzzing by the time he got himself to the main house. Fear slid along his spine as he banged on the door.

A moment later, Belle whipped it open. Her nervous glance shot over his shoulder, as if she was looking for someone else before settling back on him.

"Curran."

Her tension was palpable.

"Jane," he said, trying not to sound too distraught. He didn't want to panic her grandmother. "Where is she?"

Belle wrung her hands. "She went after her sister. Here." She pulled a note from her pocket and handed it to him. "It seems as if Susan went to meet Timothy Brady. We don't know for certain what his intentions are, but Jane followed to stop Susan."

Timothy Brady.

Curran's gut clenched. They never had caught up with the assistant trainer at Churchill Downs. What if he was dangerous, despite Jane's insistence that the man had done nothing but help her in Hudson

Valley. She might confront him with a disastrous result.

Perhaps she already had—the source of his irrational imaginings.

Why would Jane be so careless as to be forcing a face-to-face with the very man who could be after her? Curran wondered. Undoubtedly, because she didn't believe he was guilty of anything but having information about Shaw's troubles.

"The Potters' old place," he said. "Where exactly might that be?"

"Straight north of here. It's a tobacco farm."

"Maybe we should call the house and ask Mr. Potter to check on them."

"That's not possible," Belle told him. "No one lives there now. The Potters built a fancy place in Lexington last year. And their farm manager has his own home. So no one is actually on the property full-time."

"Then I shall go after them myself." Acting calmer than he was feeling, Curran took Belle's hand and squeezed reassuringly. "Try not to be worrying yourself sick, now."

"Thank you, Curran. You're so kind to us. I don't know what we would do without you."

"The feeling is mutual." Letting go of her hand, he asked, "How will I know the property?"

"After you pass the third crossroad, slow down and watch on your left for a dirt road that cuts through the tobacco field. That's it. Just head straight in."

"Can you think of any particular place where Timothy and Susan could meet?"

"I haven't been on the property for years. I remember a couple of curing barns. You have to pass them to get to the house.''

"I'll find your granddaughters, Belle, and I shall be bringing them home to you,'' he assured her.

"Godspeed.''

Jogging to his car, Curran only prayed that he was telling the truth, that his internal radar would bring him to the woman he loved before another tragedy struck.

STILL LEANING against the locked door, Jane tried to ignore the heat as she squeezed her eyes shut and concentrated.

Entering the barn...the too-dry heat...yellowing tobacco...Susan, eyes wide and panicky...

See this Curran, she thought. *Feel this.* Now, *when it really counts!*

"Jane? Are you okay?'' Susan asked, sounding weird, as if her throat weren't working properly.

As it probably wasn't due to the dry, hot air, Jane thought, trying to use as little energy as possible as she hobbled back to her sister. This time when she let herself sink down to the ground, she did so carefully.

"I'm all right and so are you,'' she said as much to convince herself as Susan. "And we're going to stay that way. Here, let me untie you.''

"I tried to warn you!''

"I know you did, sweetheart.''

Once she freed her sister, Jane gathered the teenager in her arms and hugged her tight. Susan was shaking uncontrollably.

"I'm sorry,'' she said with a sob. "I'm sorry, sorry, sorry!''

"Timothy Brady will be even sorrier when I get my hands on him," Jane vowed.

"No, not Tim. He wasn't the one," Susan gasped out, pushing at her with very little power.

Jane realized that her sister was already in a weakened state. Flushed, she appeared ready to faint. Jane wasn't feeling great herself, but she knew it might be important to get as much information as possible while they both still could talk.

"Do you know who did this to you? What did he look like?"

"I—I don't know." With a shaky hand, Susan swiped at her forehead as if something were crawling on it. "Sorry. Headache. I couldn't tell. It was already getting dark and he wore a billed cap pulled down low. I—I only saw him for a few seconds before he threw me to the ground."

Jane's chest tightened. "He hurt you?" She had to force out the words.

"Only a little while he tied me up. And then when he dragged me into the barn and threw me back here." Susan licked her parched lips. "Why did this happen to us, Jane? What's going on?"

The time for honesty was now.

Jane gave her sister the short version, and though she told the truth, including the fact that not only had Gavin tried to kill her, but someone closer to home, as well, she softened the grisly particulars as much as possible.

And she left out the personal details about Gavin.

Susan took it all in, then asked, "Does Nani know?"

"I told her this morning. That's what I was discussing with Curran when you overheard me talking about sending you off to Mother. I wasn't trying to punish you, Susan. I was trying to protect you.''

The teenager's face crumpled. ''And I just made everything worse.''

''It's my fault, not yours. You didn't know what was going on.''

''Why didn't you tell me, Jane? I'm your sister. I had a right. I love you. I don't want to lose you.''

''And I love you. I just haven't been thinking straight lately.''

Jane hugged Susan again, wondering if her sister was so enamored of Tim Brady that she was lying for him. Or perhaps it was just that she couldn't face the truth. And would rather believe it had been someone else. It was too hot to hang on to Susan for long. Jane was going to have to get her sister out of here before it was too late. She felt as if they were in an oven.

Indeed, the curing barn was an oven of sorts, and it was definitely on *Bake*.

THE IMAGE CAME to him just before he passed the second major intersection.

A pipe slashing downward...no, a cane...it battered at a wooden wall...sprayed a few chips but did minimal damage...then pain shot through his hand and heat seared him from the inside out...

Headlights flicking at him from the crossroad jerked Curran back to the drive.

''What the hell was that?''

His pulse picked up and his mouth went dry and he swore he could feel Jane, as if...as if she were inside him...as if she was trying to reach him.

Nothing like this had ever happened before. Then,

Jane—*his Sheena*—had never happened to him before.

He sped through the night, somehow knowing that Jane's very life was in his hands.

The heat was getting to him. Had he switched it on rather than the air-conditioning? He stuck his hand in front of a vent. Cold air. Puzzled, he withdrew his hand.

What in the hell was going on?

He rolled down the window for fresh air, but no matter. He couldn't seem to cool down. Weird—he was blazing hot but not sweating.

He sped through the third intersection, then slowed and soon found the dirt road. Cutting between the tobacco fields, safe from other vehicles, he concentrated on Jane.

Fear…anger…frustration…headache.

Curran…Curran…Curran…

She summoned him, but from where? And why was her presence getting weaker, as if she couldn't keep focused?

He concentrated on finding her in his mind.

He entered the void, met only dark, then pulled himself back out.

Jane must be in the abandoned house somewhere, he decided. And Susan, he could only hope that she was all right.

Glancing at the approaching twin structures—barns—Curran dismissed them and stared ahead, trying to find the house by moonlight.

Sheena, where are you? I'm coming. Help me find you!

Dry heat seared him with shocking intensity as he rolled past the twin barns, still focused on finding the old house. Increasing heat rolled down the back of his neck and along his spine. Suddenly he gasped and put on the brakes, then glanced back over his shoulder.

Pipes from what looked like a furnace snaked to the barns, no doubt supplying them with enough heat to dry the tobacco!

Sheena?

Heat sizzled his nerves.

Curran, help!

Jerking his focus onto the car, he put it in reverse and stepped on the accelerator. Practically flying backward, he waited until he was between the two barns to jam on the brakes.

Curran threw open the car door, yelling, "I'm coming, Jane, hang on!"

But which barn?

He started with the right. The door opened easily.

"Jane, are you in here?"

Listening intently, he heard not the slightest sound. Felt not the slightest connection. And the fact that the air was warm but not hot drove him to check the other building.

When he saw that the door had been jammed shut, he was certain this was it. Pulse surging, he made quick work of the simple but effective barricade.

"Jane, are you all right?" he called out.

And as the door slid open, heat blasted him so that he took a step back before entering.

"Curran, here."

He entered the maze of drying tobacco, following the direction of her voice and the flash of light coming from the back of the barn.

When he got close enough to see her, Jane was

helping her sister to her feet. Susan didn't seem to
have the strength to stay there. He swept the teenager
up into his arms, where she hung limply.

"What about you?" he asked Jane. "Will you be
all right for a moment?"

"Go. I'm fine."

"I'll get her into the car and be back for you."

Rushing Susan into the far cooler summer night,
Curran felt for her pulse. It was fast. And her skin
was not only hot to the touch, but it had lost its
elasticity. He wondered how long she'd been captive.
How hot had been hot? Enough to seriously dehydrate her, he suspected.

Carefully, he set her in the front seat and hit the
door lock, just in case whoever had done this was
still around.

"I have to leave you for a minute now."

Susan nodded. "Get Jane."

By the time Curran turned around, Jane was already in the doorway. She moved slowly and leaned
heavily on her cane, but she appeared to be in better
shape than her sister.

Overcome with relief, he wrapped his arms around
her and, when Jane clung to him fiercely, felt something within him opening wide. His heart?

"Ah, Sheena, thank God you're safe," Curran
murmured, his lips brushing her golden brown hair.

Holding her tight, he didn't ever want to let her
go.

"I'LL STAY with Susan," Jane said.

Though she had a bit of a headache, she was feeling better after drinking small amounts of water all

the way to the hospital, where the water had been replaced by a sports drink with potassium.

Susan had thrown up her water. The doctor had assured her that her sister would be fine, but at the moment, she was running a fever and her heart rate was in overdrive. The doctor had confined Susan to a hospital bed. She was hooked up to an IV—a saline drip—and would remain in the hospital until she stabilized.

"No, you won't stay, Jane Grantham!" her grandmother said. "The doctor told you to go home and get some rest, so go you will. You've had enough for today. *I'll* stay."

"Nani—"

"Don't use that tone with me. I've made up my mind." She looked to Curran, who stood quietly to the rear of the room. "You'll see that my granddaughter is all right?"

"You can count on me."

He might be speaking to her grandmother about her alone, but Jane knew they all three were included in that statement. They could all count on Curran McKenna.

She forced down the sudden lump in her throat. Finally, a man she could trust.

Thinking that both Susan and Nani would be safer here at the hospital than at home, Jane gave way. She kissed her sleeping sister's forehead, then hugged her grandmother hard.

"You stay put until you hear from Biggs," Nani said, patting her on the back. "He'll have his men combing that farm for clues at first light."

Jane nodded. Not that she was convinced the sheriff's men would find anything other than her and Susan's cars.

In addition to checking out the Potter farm for clues, Sheriff Biggs Mason meant to contact the Hudson Valley authorities about Gavin Shaw and to pick up Timothy Brady, even though Susan had maintained the assistant trainer's innocence in this matter. Biggs now knew the whole story. Rather, as much as she'd told Curran and her family. Except for her mother, that was.

Having called Mother in North Carolina but forced to leave a message on an answering machine, Jane wondered if she had gone out of town on a business trip with her new husband. If so, Jane was going to have to figure out what to do with Susan to keep her safe when the hospital released her.

Curran drove, and exhaustion claimed Jane. One minute they were leaving the hospital parking lot, the next they'd arrived at Grantham Acres. But instead of stopping at her door, he drove straight to the guest house.

"I'm not leaving you alone in that house tonight." He cut the ignition. "You'll be safer here."

Too tired to protest, still spooked from the night's misadventure, Jane didn't argue. She allowed him to take her arm and walk her inside.

In the living room, Curran sat her in an armchair and filled a glass with the sports drink. She sipped slowly but couldn't get enough of the liquid. How long would this parched feeling stay with her? she wondered. At least the headache was gone. Thank God Curran had arrived when he had or she might be in a hospital bed, too.

Which brought her to something else about which she'd been wondering.

"Curran, how did you really find Susan and me so quickly?"

This was the first chance she'd had to ask. They hadn't been alone since he'd found her. Nani had simply told her that Curran had come to the house looking for her and had seen Susan's note, but beyond that, she had no idea.

"The heat," he said.

"What do you mean?"

"I knew you were in trouble—I felt it," he explained, sounding a little surprised himself. "And then on the way to the farm, I felt the heat, too. It was as if you were directly inside me and I was experiencing what you were."

Jane swallowed hard. "That's what I was hoping for...and it worked. But how is this possible?"

"There is only one explanation I can think of." Curran appeared a bit dazed when he said, "You really *are* my fate. My destiny."

"Destiny?" Jane echoed, stunned by his wild statement.

He crossed to a side table where he picked up a leather-bound volume that appeared to be a journal. From that, he pulled an envelope of cream vellum.

"I have something I want you to read."

Jane slowly rose from her chair. "What is it?"

"When my Grandmother Moira knew she was dying, she wrote a letter to each of her nine grandchildren. This is her legacy to us all."

He pulled a creased and worn sheet from the envelope and handed it to her. Their fingers touched and Jane's pulse picked up and her chest tightened.

She reminded herself to breathe and then began to read.

> To my darling Curran,
> I leave you my love and more. Within thirty-three days of your thirty-third birthday—enough time to know what you are about—you will have in your grasp a legacy of which your dreams are made. Dreams are not always tangible things, but more often are born in the heart. Act selflessly in another's behalf, and my legacy will be yours.
>
> Your loving grandmother,
> Moira McKenna
>   P.S. Use any other inheritance from me wisely and only for good, lest you destroy yourself or those you love.

Stunned, Jane stared at the letter. *Act selflessly in another's behalf.* Isn't that what Curran had been doing since he'd stepped foot on Grantham Acres?

Was this it, then? The real thing? Wide-eyed, she met his gaze again.

"I wish I could have met her. And the letter...so beautiful...so fanciful..."

"So full of truth. The family calls the inheritance The McKenna Legacy. Turn thirty-three...fall in love...find yourself in grave danger."

"I-in love?" Jane's breath caught in her throat. "Are you?"

His right cheek dimpled with his smile. "Afraid so."

Afraid. He was *afraid* to love her.

Jane tried to keep her emotions in check so that

he couldn't sense her disappointment in the way he had phrased the response.

"The McKenna Legacy," she echoed. "So this really has come true before?"

"Ask my happily married sister Keelin when you meet her. Or my cousins—Skelly, Kathleen, Donovan. They've all gone through a trial by fire to be with their soul mates."

Jane's heart began to beat wildly. "Soul mates? Is that what we are?"

Curran moved closer. "What else would you call what we share? As I have told you, Sheena, I've never connected like this with another human being, only you." He ran his knuckles over her cheek. "And it seems that, between us, the gift is somehow shared or I wouldn't have been able to sense your emotions as I did tonight."

Unable to resist his gentling touch, Jane closed her eyes. "I tried to get us out. I couldn't. I didn't know what else to do, so I concentrated and thought of you. I was so afraid you wouldn't hear me."

"I shall always hear you, my Sheena."

Curran slid a hand around the back of her neck. Slowly, she opened her eyes to gaze into his. They came closer. So close that his features blurred. And then it didn't matter because he was kissing her and she let her lids drift close.

Her limbs lost their little strength and she swayed against Curran. She couldn't help herself—she felt her defenses crumbling. And then Curran surrounded her with himself.

Jane wrapped her arms around his waist and clung to him, her head light and heart soaring. His heat pressed in on her, but this time it was a good heat and she was drawn to it, wanted more of it, demanded it. Working her hands across the material of his shirt, she explored the muscles in his lower back with her fingertips.

"I need you, Sheena," he murmured against her mouth.

Moaning, she rocked against him in agreement.

Curran deepened the kiss and slid his hands slowly down her sides and over her hips. Then he cupped her bottom and pulled her snugly into him so that she could feel the enormity of that need for her.

Wet heat flushed through her and she nestled closer. His heart beat so fiercely she could feel the rapid palpitation against her own chest. Her own heart responded in kind. And her breasts grew heavy and ached for his touch. As if he read her mind—and he very well might have, she thought through a haze of desire—he worked one hand upward to the fullness of sensitive flesh that only one man before him had ever handled. She moved in his arms slightly to allow him access, and at his first touch, her knees gave way.

Curran caught her and swung her up into his arms as easily as he had her much lighter sister earlier.

"I'll be taking you upstairs, if you don't mind."

But he didn't move until she shook her head and whispered, "I'll not mind a bit."

She wrapped her arms around his neck as he carried her to the staircase, and once he stepped up, he began kissing her again. Not deep full kisses, but light exchanges that set her lips to tingling.

Then he substituted her chin for her lips, then her throat, her chest, her breasts. By the time he got to the landing, she was tingling all over.

Once in his bedroom, he lay her across the king-size bed and continued downward, unbuttoning and unzipping her trousers as he distracted her with his mouth.

But when he freed her for a moment, Jane froze. Her knee—no one but the medical team had seen the awful mess of her knee since the surgery.

But the lights were low, she thought nervously. Perhaps he wouldn't even notice.

Curran tugged off her shoes, then rolled her trousers over her hips and down her legs, leaving her vulnerable. But he continued kissing her. Her stomach, her inner thigh. Her knee. For a moment, he lingered there, gently stroking her leg, caressing and kissing the very scar she had been trying so hard to hide.

Fearing his pity, Jane bit her lip.

Curran moved upward, his kisses leaving tiny stings that traveled along her nerves to her center. Forgetting her trepidation, she arched. He kissed her through her sensible cotton panties. With his teeth, he caught the edge and pulled them lower, exposing her bit by bit so slowly that she thought she would scream if he didn't hurry.

"Tell me what you might be wanting, Sheena," he whispered.

She answered with a little moan.

Suddenly Curran plunged upward and lay half over her, his knee in the crevice of her thighs, his erection pressed into her hip. "I do not think you were quite clear enough on that," he said, unbuttoning her blouse with one hand.

"You're intuitive." She began undoing his shirt, as well. "Look into my mind."

"I want to hear the words."

Gazing deeply into his eyes, she thought, *Take me, Curran. Make love to me. Be true to me. Love me.*

His eyes widened, but he didn't say a word, merely finished undressing them both in record time.

Nude and vulnerable, she gave herself over to sensation, following his lead as he explored her body and she his. Restless, wanting more, she spread her legs and pressed herself against him. He explored her there, too, opening her folds with gentle fingers, then manipulating her wet sex until her heart pounded in her ears. Every time he brought her to the brink of a climax, he backed off until she began to writhe in agony in a surfeit of frustrated passion.

Slowly, he dipped a finger deep inside her. Then two. Unable to help herself, she rode them.

What do you want, Sheena?

You inside me.

In one smooth motion, he withdrew his fingers and straddled her, careful to avoid her left knee, then slipped inside her and stopped.

Breathing hard, she tried to stop, too. Tried to savor the moment. But nearly crazed with need, she couldn't. She moved under him, raising her hips so she moved along his length. Now it was she pressing her palms against his bottom, pulling him closer until she couldn't tell where she ended and he began.

Panting, she watched his face. Closed eyes. Tight expression. Slightly parted lips.

He was breathing hard. Ready.

So was she.

She slipped one hand in between their bodies and found him.

When her fingertips touched him, he groaned, "Ah-h, Sheena, you've undone me."

Jane closed her eyes and let go of her last bit of control. Curran rode her to ecstasy, and they shuddered long and hard before touching down together.

For a moment, their hearts beat as one. Jane floated, loving Curran's weight pinning her to the bed. She wanted more. She wanted everything from him.

For a little while, at least, she would allow herself to be ridiculously happy.

When Curran rolled onto his side, he brought her with him, kept her close against his chest. Sighing, she fit herself to him and slipped an arm around his waist.

He stroked her hair loose around her shoulders. "I don't know what I would have done had I not been on time tonight—"

"But you were."

"—because I can no longer imagine life without you."

Nor she without him. Not that she said so. Everything was too new. Too frightening.

And once again, too fast.

His fate, Curran had called her. His destiny. Could it be true? Was he the one? Or was he controlled by the tale of The McKenna Legacy?

More important, was she once more being foolish enough to believe what she wanted to hear? For she had wanted to hear all he'd had to say to her and more.

It had been different with Gavin, Jane told herself. She'd been attracted to him, had formed an attachment, had agreed to make a comfortable, familiar life with him. But her decisions had been, or so she'd thought, rational. And practical.

But with Curran, she could hardly think straight when he was near her. And when he used his gentling touch...

She didn't know if they had a future. Certainly not if her nameless nemesis had anything to say about it. She couldn't so easily shake off the doubts that her experience with Gavin had instilled in her.

Jane feared that, for the first time in her life, she was deeply, madly, truly in love, and that was the scariest thing that had ever happened to her.

Chapter Thirteen

Dawn's pale light was spilling into the room when Curran awakened and reached for his Sheena, as he had twice during the night. But her side of the bed was empty.

Thinking she might be in the bathroom, he called, "Jane?" but she didn't answer.

Pulse jagging, Curran sat straight up and looked around the room. Jane's clothes were gone.

Leaving his bed, he crossed to the stairway. Though no lights were on below, he called out again. "Jane, are you downstairs?" Again, no answer. "Damn!"

What had she been thinking to go off on her own? She could be in danger.

Quickly, Curran started dressing.

Why had she left? *Susan.* If Jane had called the hospital and had gotten negative information about her sister, surely she would have awakened him.

What, then?

Another unpleasant thought bushwhacked him. An unpleasant memory of Maggie. She had always insisted on his leaving her bed before daybreak so that no one would guess that they were sleeping together. Had Jane left his bed for the same reason?

Remembering his suspicions about her covert relationship with Shaw, Curran couldn't shake the notion. Displeasure stiffened his fingers as he buttoned his shirt. He wandered over to the bedroom window and looked out to the main house. Her car was still there. He continued staring as if he could connect with her.

And perhaps he could.

But as hard as he concentrated, nothing. No emotions to capture. Perhaps she had fallen asleep again.

About to turn away, Curran froze when a furtive movement from below caught his attention. Someone down there was skulking around the house, peering into the first-floor windows. Not enough light to identify the person.

His pulse raced faster than his feet could carry him down the stairs. He shot out the front door and jogged toward the main house, praying he could get there to prevent any further hurt to the woman he loved.

The intruder was still poised outside the kitchen window and peering in.

Curran slowed and willed his breathing to do the same so that he wouldn't alert the bastard. Silently, he sneaked up on the man who was wearing dark pants, a tweed jacket and a hat jammed low on his head.

A familiar hat below which Curran spotted a few strands of red. "Ned!" he yelled. "What the bloody hell do you think you are about?"

His assistant trainer jumped and turned to face him. "Curran, lad, you gave me a start." He visibly tried to compose himself. "I—I was looking for you."

Curran remembered catching Ned coming out of his own quarters and the refrain had been the same. "You were looking for me in the main house at daybreak and spying through the windows at that?"

"I-it's so early that I didn't want to wake anyone."

"Liar!" Curran grabbed the man by his jacket front and spun him around and into a tree trunk. "Start talking, Ned, before I beat it out of you."

"You wouldn't!" Ned's bushy red eyebrows raised and his pale eyes widened. "Calm down, Curran. You're not a violent man by nature."

"Try me," Curran threatened, thinking of what they'd gone through the night before. Ned would have to convince him that he wasn't involved. "If you want to keep your face intact, then talk."

Ned hesitated only a second before caving. "All right, all right. I was hired to keep an eye on you and the Grantham woman, that's all. To report your activities. How the stallion was coming along. That sort of thing."

To report Jane's movements, Curran mused, so that someone else could ambush her?

"I can guarantee you that Finn mac Cumhail has never been in that house."

"Please, Curran, I'm telling the truth," Ned pleaded. "I've done nothing but take a few extra punts in exchange for simple information."

"And who might be putting those punts in your pocket?"

"Don't make me do this."

"Either you tell me or I turn you over to Sheriff

Mason,'' Curran said. ''Someone locked Jane and Susan in a curing barn last night and left them to die. You're as good a suspect as any.''

Ned's normally ruddy face went ashen, and Curran could feel the man tremble where he still held him fixed against the tree trunk.

''Murder? You think I'm a murderer? No, Curran, in God's name, I swear it wasn't me. I did nothing but a little reconnaissance, now, and that's the sum of it.''

Ned was an emotional time bomb. Curran could sense it. And though he concentrated, though he was physically touching the man, he couldn't get in.

He could only do that with the woman who was his fate.

And still, Curran was certain that Ned told the truth. He also sensed that Ned was no murderer.

''Give me a name,'' Curran demanded of him.

''I can't.''

''If you value your own skin, you will!''

Red-faced, Ned banged the back of his own head against the tree twice. Then he sighed and gave it up. ''Timothy Brady.''

Which didn't exactly surprise Curran. He'd had his suspicions about Brady all along. He pulled Ned toward him, then shoved the man away. Ned stumbled but caught himself from falling.

''So it's been Brady all along.''

''Aye. I'm sorry, Curran.''

Sorry for himself, Curran thought. Sorry that he'd been caught. But sorry that he'd been bribed to spy? Doubtful.

''You'll be even sorrier, Ned, when word gets out that you're a man who can't be trusted.''

"You'll ruin me over this?"

"What did you think I would do? Pat you on the back, tell you, 'That's all right, lad, everything will be jake,' and send you on your way?"

"But if Tim knows I gave him up...and you say he's a murderer..."

"Then you'd best be fast," Curran suggested. "Pack your things and get out before he can catch you."

"You're firing me?"

"Now you have it." He couldn't believe Ned would think otherwise. "Be off Grantham Acres before I come to check that you've cleared out."

Curran turned his back on the traitor.

"Wait!" Ned protested. "What about my airline ticket back to Shannon?"

"What about it?" Clenching his jaw, Curran turned back toward Ned. "Use the money you've been paid to spy on getting yourself home."

Scowling at him, Ned jammed his hat down hard on his head and stalked off toward his own quarters without so much as a glance backward.

A man with a grudge could be dangerous, Curran mused. Then, again, the authorities were involved, which should give Ned pause if he was considering revenge. Thinking that he would suggest that Sheriff Mason question Ned as well as Brady, he waited until his former assistant was out of sight before moving toward the house.

Jane was standing at the window, watching. Had she seen the whole interchange?

Curran stopped for a moment and stared. He tried to read her. Nothing. He felt neither gladness to see him nor dismay. Apparently Jane had found a way to keep him out.

At least out of her mind, Curran thought, heading for the house, his feelings mixed.

On the one hand, he wanted to sweep her up in his arms and hold her out of sheer gratitude that she was all right. On the other, he was disappointed and a bit irate that she'd up and left his bed before daybreak. And so, he approached her warily.

She met him in the foyer, asking without preamble, "What was that all about?"

No greeting. No words of affection. And her body language was no more encouraging, Curran thought. She was holding herself straight and stiff. Inaccessible.

In response, he held himself back. He didn't even try to keep the coolness from his tone when he said, "That was about Ned's spying on us and reporting back to Timothy Brady."

"What!"

"And then I fired him, told him to leave immediately."

"He's going now? Biggs might want to talk to him."

"And I'll be informing Sheriff Mason about our conversation, though I doubt Ned knows anything of value. But Mason will be wanting to pick up Brady for certain."

"You don't think…last night…"

"That Brady tried to kill you? Why not?"

"Because Susan swore Tim wasn't there."

"Are you certain she wasn't trying to protect him?"

"Oh, Lord, I hope not." Though the morning air

was comfortable, Jane rubbed her arms as if she was chilled. "I guess I just can't trust my own judgment ever."

Curran saw his opening to change the subject to one more personal when he heard a car engine. He glanced out the narrow window at the side of the door.

"That's Belle now."

"What is she doing here?" Jane didn't wait for her grandmother to come in. Instead, she threw open the front door and moved to the car, her limp barely noticeable this morning. "Nani? How is Susan?"

"Your sister is fine." Belle looked over her granddaughter and gave her a big hug. "Her temperature is normal and her heart rate stabilized." She glanced at Curran when she said, "I'm just here to pack a few things for us, then I'll go back to the hospital to get Susan. Mitzi Driver said she will be happy to have us for a few days."

Jane sighed. "I'm so glad you thought of asking one of your friends. I was worried about bringing Susan back home."

"That invitation includes you, Jane."

Belle started for the house, Jane following, protesting, "Me? I can't go."

"Udell and Jimi can take care of the horses for a few days until Biggs gets his man."

"And in the meantime, you want me to bring trouble to Mitzi's?" Jane shook her head. "I have to stay here, Nani, and see this through."

"She has a valid point." Following them back inside the foyer, Curran flicked a glance at Jane, who seemed to be avoiding looking at him more than she had to. "And I shall be here to protect her."

Though perhaps not as closely as he might like to. "I'm going to ask Biggs to post one of his men here, as well," Belle insisted.

"If that will ease your mind," Curran said, after which he told Belle all about Ned and Timothy Brady.

"Oh, dear, Susan is going to be very upset."

"I know." Jane sighed. "She believes he's innocent. At least she said he wasn't the one who locked us in the curing barn. No description. Not very helpful, I'm afraid."

"Ned. Tim. A mystery man, if Susan was truthful with you," Belle muttered. "Do you think she was being honest?"

"I just don't know. Maybe she believes it was someone else."

"That would mean we have a conspiracy," Belle said. "To what end?"

"Finn mac Cumhail." Curran couldn't quite piece it together. "It must go back to the stallion."

All three fell silent and thoughtful.

Curran flicked his gaze to Jane, who was acting as if last night had never happened. She stood closer to Belle than to him, and she had turned her shoulder in a *don't approach* posture. She reminded him of Finn after he'd won a victory over the stallion. Finn would always regress a bit as if to assert his independence. Is that what Jane was doing?

Suddenly she asked him, "What do you know about Mukhtar Saladin and Holt Easterling?"

"Easterling and I have a serious difference in training methods," he said. "He has a cruel streak that I can't tolerate. I've seen him use force on his horses."

"What about on people?"

"He isn't what you would call a pleasant man. Other than that?" He shrugged. "As for Saladin—at the party, he warned me away from Finn for my own good, said working with him could be dangerous. As a matter of fact, when I ran into him, Easterling warned me, as well, said he would do whatever he must to see that Stonehenge won the Classic."

"That sounds pretty damning," Belle said. "Either man could have been the one with murderous intent last night."

"I vote for Saladin myself," Jane offered. "He seems so solicitous of Phyllis, but she's afraid of him."

"Phyllis Singleton-Volmer is no victim," Belle stated firmly. "She's always been a sly one, from the time she was a girl. At the party, she spoke as if she were great friends with your mother in school, but she was very competitive with Lydia. Actually, they were rivals."

"Over what?"

Just then, the telephone rang.

Jane's eyes went wide. "Who could be calling at this hour? The hospital?"

"Don't panic." Belle reached for the telephone. "I told you, Susan is just fine." She put the receiver to her ear. "Hello." She listened a moment, then her eyebrows shot up. "Yes, Biggs, they're both standing right here. Hold on." She looked from Curran to Jane. "Biggs is with his officers at the Potters' curing barns. He asked if the two of you could meet him there as soon as possible."

Wondering why the sheriff wanted them to return

to the scene of the crime, Curran said, "Tell him we're on our way."

Jane sat stiffly in the passenger seat, uncomfortable despite the perfect morning. She didn't ever want to step foot on the Potters' farm again and here she was speeding back toward it. Rather, Curran was the one speeding. And silent.

A chill shot through her.

What was wrong with her? Why couldn't she say something to break the ice? Her own insecurities were driving a wedge between them.

This wasn't the way two people were supposed to act after they made love for the first time.

"Here we are," he said, slowing to make the turn.

Her fault, Jane thought. She shouldn't have left without waking him. Blasted with insecurity, she had made her escape. But perhaps she had been right in doing so, she thought, giving his hard profile a sideways glance.

She wished for the Curran she knew—charming, wheedling, gentling her?

In his place was a cold, hard stranger.

The twin barns loomed closer and she saw Sheriff Biggs Mason standing outside his vehicle, talking to a uniformed officer. The place was crawling with deputies.

Curran stopped the car, and as they climbed out, Biggs came over to greet them. He was a bit younger than Nani, just this side of retirement, as evidenced by a shock of white hair and skin as tough and wrinkled as leather left out in the sun too long. He was also whipcord thin, in better condition than most men twenty years his junior.

"Got here mighty fast," he said, raising white eyebrows. "A lawman might think you were speeding."

"We're the guys in the white hats," Curran countered, "come to give the authorities aid."

Biggs winked at Jane. "Got a smooth-tongued one there, huh?"

"Very smooth," she agreed.

She felt Curran's gaze on her. If he thought he was going to force a connection, he had another think coming. She focused on Biggs and what he had to say.

"I had my boys go over this place with a fine-tooth comb. Found your cars over there in that brush," he said, pointing to a spot farther along the road.

And from the brush, a red light was flashing.

"What's going on down there?" Jane asked, her trepidation building.

"We found something else, as well," Biggs added. "I gotta warn you, it ain't pretty."

"What isn't?"

"A body. Murder victim."

"Murder..." Her heart began to thump wildly. "Who?"

"That's what I hoped one of you might tell us. It's likely he had something to do with what happened to you last night. No identification on the body. And if he's local, my boys don't know him."

Jane finally looked to Curran, but he, too, was unreadable. His expression was deliberately neutral.

"How did he die?" he asked.

"Blunt instrument to the head. Tire iron. Told you it wasn't pretty."

Biggs had them climb into his vehicle, then drove them to the scene of the crime. By the time they arrived a few minutes later, Jane's stomach was tied in knots. The flashing lights belonged to an ambulance and the driver and paramedic stood around waiting with a stretcher.

The sheriff led the way past two of his men and a woman taking photographs. It all seemed to happen in slow motion. People moving aside. Her moving toward the body…looking down…blinking in horror.

"So can you do it?" Biggs asked. "Can you identify the victim?"

Jane nodded and once again in unison with Curran said, "Timothy Brady."

BIGGS FOLLOWED THEM back to Grantham Acres. As they entered the house, Nani was just bringing two overnight bags down the stairs. She set them next to the staircase.

"I guess Susan can wait a while longer. So what did you find?"

"Timothy Brady," Curran told her. "Dead."

Her hand fluttered to her heart. "Dear Lord."

"So Susan was undoubtedly telling the truth about Tim *not* being the one to lock us in the curing barn," Jane said. "Whoever killed him must have."

"Let's go sit," Nani said.

Her grandmother ushered them into the parlor. Jane chose her usual chair and Curran sat across the room from her. Even so, she could feel him staring. Her nerve endings tingling, she met his gaze.

For a moment, it was there—the connection. Warmth flowed through her and she wanted to say something to narrow the breach, but of course she couldn't, not with other people around. She turned away and forced her attention on Biggs.

"But Brady was also obviously involved," he was saying, "or he wouldn't have been at the Potter farm to begin with."

Jane shook her head. That she hadn't been able to believe it was yet more proof of her poor judgment.

"I don't understand," she said. "Tim was so helpful. He took care of everything after Finn and I were almost killed."

"About that," Biggs said. "I heard back from the Hudson Valley sheriff's office. Gavin Shaw's death was never reported."

"What?" Jane whispered, stunned.

"What about the other law enforcement agencies?" Curran asked.

"The man who spoke to me—Sheriff Lathrop—was thorough. Nothing."

"No wonder they never found the body." Jane's guilt returned, twofold. She'd thought she'd done the right thing, but again, she'd been fooled. "No one looked. Those detectives were fakes. But why would Tim have set me up like that?"

"We may never know."

"We will if I have anything to say about it," Jane said.

Biggs took down the description of the supposed detective who had questioned her about Shaw's death. "You haven't ever run into him away from Hudson Valley?"

"No, never. Why didn't I see it?" she asked. "Tim's taking care of everything was just too smooth, especially the part about bringing the Hudson Valley authorities to the emergency room."

Visualizing the scene, she saw again the detective pacing the corridor. And then it struck her. He'd had bushy red eyebrows.

"Ned!" she said with a gasp. "Now I know why he looked so familiar. I thought I had seen him at a racetrack, but it was the hospital. He was one of the supposed detectives. I remember seeing him in the corridor."

Curran had already filled Biggs in on Ned's spying on them and his connection to Tim. And the sheriff had hurriedly sent one of his officers to detain Ned, but the assistant trainer had already disappeared.

Now it seemed that he had done more for money than just spy on them.

Did that include murder?

Biggs went over everything again, from Gavin's attack on her to their theory that Saladin or Easterling might have locked them in the curing barn.

"Owners and trainers have been known to cheat to win," Biggs said. "But murder is a bit drastic, especially since you have nothing that could be used against them."

"But they don't know that," Jane said.

"I think they would," Biggs countered. "Rather, whoever is behind the whole thing would. No doubt, that's why you were set up in the E.R. with fake police. To find out what you knew. They had to be satisfied with your answers. If they intended to kill you, they would have done so before you left Hudson Valley."

Whoever *they* were, Jane thought, her head whirling with the complexity of it all. Under the instructions of someone else, Tim had set her up to make sure she didn't know something. What? And then that person had killed Tim. Why? And it all went back to Finn mac Cumhail.

By the time Biggs left, Jane was drained of emotion except for a growing anger at all she'd had to endure these past months. She couldn't just sit around and wait for answers. She would find some herself.

A plan growing in her mind, she refused to think it through in Curran's presence lest he latch on to her thoughts and try to stop her.

"Nani, I won't have a car for the moment, it's being held for evidence in Tim's murder. Fingerprints and the like. What if I drive you and Susan to Mitzi's and then use your car."

"Excellent idea, sweetheart. Mitzi will get us anywhere we need to go."

"I can come along," Curran said.

Jane snapped, "That won't be necessary. You need to work with Finn, remember?"

And she needed to be free of him for a while so that she could continue to think straight.

Anger flared through Curran's features before he masked it and said, "Belle, would you give us a few minutes alone. We need to talk strategy."

Obviously he wasn't okay with her plan.

Nani looked from him to her and raised her eyebrows. "Certainly. I'll be out in the car." She picked up the overnight bags.

"I'll get those," Curran offered.

"No need. I'm not infirm yet."

The moment her grandmother was out the front door, Curran turned on Jane.

"Tell me," he asked coolly, "what happened to you at dawn? Did you turn into another person?"

Immediately put off, she snapped, "I am who I am, Curran."

He stared at her and she wished for all the world that he would take her in his arms and tell her that he really did love her. That he hadn't said the words just to get her into bed. To trick her somehow.

"What makes you so afraid?"

"You do!"

She'd never felt so vulnerable. Part of her knew she and Curran belonged together, but another part was certain she'd made another mistake.

"I do," Curran repeated. "Is that because I've been so cruel to you...or because you're afraid of what people will say?"

"W-what?"

"I told you before that you're a snob. I guess I was right."

"How dare you judge me!"

"How dare you treat me like I'm invisible. I've had enough of that!"

"I don't—"

"Maggie Butler hid our relationship from her society friends, from racing people, even from her own family. And I let her do it because I was crazy about her. I mistakenly believed that once she realized that I was more than a bed partner to her, things would change. Only they never did. She fired me and threw me out rather than embarrass herself in front of her peers."

"I'm not—"

Riding over her protest, he said, "I'm not that man anymore. I won't take that kind of treatment, not from anyone, not even from the woman I love!"

With that, Curran whipped around and strode to the front door.

"Wait a minute!" Jane protested, realizing that he'd said it again—that he loved her. "You've got it all wrong."

"Who are you willing to tell about us, Jane? Your grandmother? Your sister?" When she didn't answer fast enough, he muttered, "That's what I thought," and left, slamming the door closed behind him.

A stunned Jane stared at the door, mind whirling.

In his own way, Curran McKenna was as insecure as she was. Only he didn't know why she was so reluctant to be open and free with him. It had nothing to do with who he was or what he did for a living.

That he thought her a snob hurt.

That he hadn't given her the chance to explain how she felt was even worse.

Chapter Fourteen

By the time they'd had a chat with Susan and told her about Tim—she was understandably upset, if not devastated—Jane had formulated a plan. She waited until she rolled up to Mitzi Driver's house and stopped the car, then turned to talk to her sister.

"Susan, do you by any chance know where Tim was staying? Biggs needs that information."

A dark expression crossed Susan's young face. "Rolling Meadows, along with his bosses."

Staying at Phyllis's farm and Phyllis didn't know who he was? Or had she just been evasive when they'd asked her about him at Churchill Downs the day before. Why?

"Was Tim staying at the house?"

"No. He had a room, part of the rear barn."

With that, Susan opened her door and escaped any further conversation. Not so their grandmother.

"Jane, dear, tell me you're not going to do anything foolish."

"I've been foolish enough as it is, Nani. It's time I smartened up."

Especially about men, she thought, her argument with Curran still stinging.

"Jane—"

"Don't concern yourself about me, please. Just take good care of Susan until Biggs has this thing wrapped up."

Her grandmother sank back into a silence of disapproval. Jane hated it when they argued. She hated the silent treatment even more.

"Come on, Nani, let me help you get the bags inside."

This time the older woman didn't quibble.

A few minutes later, Jane was on the road again. Nani knew her too well. Rather than driving home, she headed straight for Rolling Meadows Farm.

Alone, she couldn't help but think of Curran. She really wasn't a snob. But she was constantly questioning her own feelings. And her every decision. She would have to tell Curran the personal details involving Gavin and explain how he'd made her distrust herself. Maybe then he would understand.

Upon her arrival at Phyllis's farm ten minutes later, she had the presence of mind to avoid the main house, easily done by taking a gravel side road around the property. The barns soon shifted into view. She drew opposite the barn set farthest to the rear and parked near the three-board, black fence.

Taking stock before she did anything, Jane noted several workers, but all were busy around the barn closest to the house. No one nearby. Good.

Her pulse threaded unevenly as she left the car. Knowing emotions were a no-no—Curran might sense them—she focused on the barn and the door that looked as if it might open to living quarters. Squeezing through the boards was tricky, but easier for her than climbing over the fence. Then, using her cane more for balance than support, she crossed the expanse of grass to the barn.

She was nearly to the building when a man came through the open front double doors. Holt Easterling! And it took him only a moment to spot her.

He stopped, scowled, then stalked toward her, demanding, "What are you doing here?"

Watching his expression carefully to see if it changed, she said, "I'm here to see Tim. I need to talk to him about my sister, Susan."

He glanced from her to the closed door she'd already targeted and shrugged. "As long as you don't cause trouble. And when you're done talking, tell him I expect him to report to work immediately."

"Fine," she said, breathing easily once more.

The trainer walked away without so much as a backward glance. Did that mean he was innocent? Jane wondered. He acted as if he thought Tim was alive and sleeping in. If he really believed that, then he wasn't the mystery man, and obviously, Biggs hadn't gotten around to questioning him yet. She suspected the sheriff would get around to him soon enough.

Luckily, Tim's door was unlocked. Inside, she flicked on the wall switch and regarded the modest quarters—a sort of studio apartment with a kitchenette. Plain but clean.

She started with the dressers. Not much on top, so she checked the drawers. Nothing that pointed him to a life of crime.

Disappointed, she opened his closet door and stared at the few garments hanging on the single rack. She began checking the pockets. From one pair of pants, she pulled a piece of gum. From another a peppermint candy. But the only thing in the top pocket of the suit jacket was a folded slip of paper.

When she unfolded it, Jane gasped. It was a check made out for five thousand dollars. And it was signed by Phyllis Singleton-Volmer herself. It could be a paycheck, she supposed, but how could Phyllis pretend not to know Tim when she was signing his checks.

Jane's hand shook as she stuffed the check into her own pocket. Evidence, she thought. But for what? Services rendered, but were they professional? Personal? Or illegal?

If only Curran were here, he might have some ideas. She was beginning to regret dismissing him so hastily. And she was feeling guilty. He'd been with her all the way, after all.

What now?

Jane thought about it and decided she was going to talk to Phyllis. Perhaps she could be as persistent as the society woman and wring some bit of information out of her. When she opened the door, her jaw dropped. Phyllis herself was standing there, reaching for the door handle.

"Jane!" Phyllis started. "What in the world…" She got hold of herself and pulled her mouth into a smile. "Imagine meeting you here, of all places."

"Imagine."

"What are you doing here?"

"As I told Mr. Easterling, I came to talk to Tim about my sister."

"But you can't. I mean, he's not here right now. So what are you doing in his quarters?"

"If you know he's not here, what are *you* doing coming into his room?"

"Not that I need to explain anything to you," Phyllis said sweetly, "I came to take care of something."

"Was it this?" Heart pounding, Jane decided to go fishing. She pulled the check from her pocket. "Were you going to destroy evidence that you hired Tim?"

Phyllis's Southern charm quickly dropped. "You have as much nerve as that uppity Lydia."

Jane's pulse shot into overdrive. She'd hit a nerve. "I thought you were fond of my mother."

Phyllis froze for a moment and started to say something. Then, as if changing her mind, she narrowed her gaze at Jane, and her expression was spite-filled.

"No, actually, that was your father I was fond of. And Frederick was deeply enamored of me, as well, but Lydia didn't care that he and I were the perfect couple. She seduced him anyway. *I* should have been mistress of Grantham Acres. Not that slut. She didn't care about the farm, just about the social status it would give her. And the money it would put in her pocket, of course."

Highly offended for her mother, Jane asked, "Are you certain you're not speaking of yourself?"

"How dare you! I'm not the one who got myself pregnant to get what I wanted. Oh, you didn't know that, did you?"

Jane was speechless in the face of the accusation. Not that she believed her mother would do such a thing for money and position. Her mother had loved her father deeply.

"After Frederick died, Lydia didn't even care enough for the farm to stay and work it," Phyllis went on. "Instead, she turned it over to you, remarried and left Kentucky for good."

"And so you what?" Jane could hardly get her breath. "You decided to destroy the only thing that could keep Grantham Acres going? You, who supposedly adores horses, wants Finn mac Cumhail dead—and me—all over an old hatred for something that happened a lifetime ago?"

"You? Now your imagination is getting to you." Phyllis waved the idea away. "But the thought of Lydia's daughter losing Grantham Acres is a delicious one."

"I don't intend to lose the farm," Jane informed her. "By the way, how did you get to Gavin?"

Phyllis looked her square in the eye and asked, "Who?"

"Or was he Tim's choice?" she went on. "You do remember Tim Brady now, don't you? You are standing in his room. Of course, he's only a memory since someone murdered him."

Phyllis blanched at that. "I—I don't know what kind of a game you're playing—"

"I just want the truth, Phyllis." Movement from the doorway caught Jane's attention, but she tried not to betray the fact. "If Grantham Acres wasn't your target, why did you want Finn's legs broken?"

"I never said that."

Someone was out there. Curran? She decided to continue pressing the issue and hoped the woman would confess.

"You never denied it, either. Come on, Phyllis. I know you're dying to throw it in my face."

HAVING SPOTTED Jane's car, Curran was racing toward the barns. The call from Belle had put fear in his gut. If something had happened to Jane...

"You!" came an indignant shout. Mukhtar Saladin pointed ~~an accusatory~~ finger. "Stop, McKenna, before I have you arrested for trespassing."

Curran kept moving toward the open door in the rear barn. "I'm not the one they'll arrest. Timothy Brady has been murdered."

The Saudi owner kept pace right behind him. Raised voices drifted out from the room.

"Well," a woman said, "I will admit I wanted Finn mac Cumhail out of the race."

Phyllis. Heart thumping, Curran let caution guide him. He signaled Saladin and put his finger to his lips.

"So you're saying you wanted Stonehenge to win badly enough to destroy Finn," Jane said. "Was he that big a threat?"

Thank God she was all right, Curran thought, holding himself back from rushing in there before she got what she was after. Saladin stood stiffly at his shoulder.

"The Irish Thoroughbred had beat Stonehenge before."

"But what is it to *you?*" Jane asked. "He belongs to your lover."

"But I'm the one who chose him. And when Stonehenge wins…well, Mukhtar promised to marry me."

Saladin pushed past Curran and into the room. "I think not. I would never marry a woman who has this disrespect for a noble animal."

"Mukhtar, darling, no—"

"I heard everything, Phyllis."

"You heard false accusations."

"I heard the truth in your voice. I want nothing more to do with you except perhaps to see that justice is served."

"Now you'll have to do your talking to Sheriff Biggs Mason," Curran told her. "He'll especially want to know what you had to do with Timothy Brady's murder."

"Murder?" Phyllis sounded truly horrified. She looked from him to Jane. "You're insane, both of you!"

Curran said, "The sheriff is on his way here now."

"I'll simply deny everything!" Phyllis shoved past them to get out the door.

"Face it," Jane called after her. "You're through now that we're on to you."

Saladin started out the door, then turned to Jane. "I must make my apologies to you, if your stallion or you were hurt in my name."

"Accepted."

And then Curran was left alone with her. He wanted in the worst way to take her in his arms, but she didn't seem particularly glad to see him.

"Is that really it, then?" Jane murmured, sounding a bit stunned.

"There's a matter of the authorities taking her in, questioning and hopefully arresting her."

"She never actually admitted anything, Curran, other than wanting to see Finn out of the race."

"Mason is a professional. He'll get the rest out of her."

"Will he? What if there is more to it than she knows? Remember, a man locked Susan and me in the curing barn. He's the one who killed Tim. Phyllis was paying Tim directly, by the way.''

She showed him the check.

''Evidence,'' he said.

''Maybe Phyllis doesn't even know about the other man. Maybe everything went through Tim. She doesn't like dirtying her hands with people who work for her.'' Jane met his gaze directly. ''But that's not me, Curran. I'm not Phyllis. Nor am I Maggie Butler.''

''Jane, about what I said before—''

''Curran, if you don't mind, I have some thinking to do before we go into it.''

''If that's how you feel.''

Her gaze met his, and he saw a great sorrow in her expression. Though tempted to tap in to their connection, he dared not. She would know.

And she would hate it.

He didn't want her to hate him…

''I promise we'll talk,'' she said softly. ''I'm just not up to it now. Or here.''

''All right, then.''

Feeling lost as he did so, Curran stepped back and let her go.

What else could he do?

A dark cloud followed him back to Grantham Acres as they sped toward the farm in separate cars. He couldn't help but think Jane was right about Phyllis. The society woman hadn't threatened her physically. She might be scheming and not above having a Thoroughbred hurt to get what she wanted, but murder was quite another thing.

As to Jane herself…

What would she have to say to him? he wondered.

Especially considering her remark about not being another Maggie Butler. His earlier accusation had stung, then. He only hoped he had been in the wrong.

After making certain Jane got into her home safely, he went back to working with Finn, who by this time was fully tacked and seeming content with it.

When Jimi got in the saddle and the stallion didn't so much as protest, he should have felt a greater sense of triumph. But his satisfaction was tempered with worry that there was more to the puzzle than they had yet defined.

Who in the world was the mystery man who had locked Jane and Susan in the curing barn?

"That's it for today," he told Jimi. "Udell, remove the tack and put him back in his stall." The groom had been standing there watching, his pride in his son evident in his big grin. "Tomorrow, we'll see how he takes to your handling rather than mine."

"Yes, sir."

If father and son had any doubts about taking the afternoon off, they didn't object. Udell said something about spending the time off with Melisande.

At least he would get to be with the woman he loved.

From the barn, Curran circled back to the main house. Belle's car was still there, but no sign of Jane. Or anyone else. No doubt she was lying low. Tempted again to force the issue with her, he held back. She would tell him when she was ready to speak of it.

Once at the guest house, he called the *Lexington Record* only to learn that Sean Harris was not at his desk but at lunch. When he identified himself, the receptionist suggested he might find the reporter at a Lexington pub called The Old Stables.

Curran hesitated only a minute before calling Jane.

"I'm going into Lexington to find Sean Harris. How soon can you be ready to leave?"

"I'm not going anywhere," she said, sounding weary. "I'm lying down and plan to stay here."

"But I'll be gone an hour or so—"

"Then go. I'll be fine. Biggs should be here soon, anyway."

"He called?"

"A little while ago."

Torn, Curran said, "Promise me you'll stay in the house and keep the doors locked."

"Curran, just go."

Instinct told him talking to Harris would fill in some piece of the puzzle, so he left, vowing to return as quickly as possible.

THE OLD STABLES SAT near the city limits, formerly part of an estate that had been broken up for mixed-use development. The long limestone building really was a former horse stable, much like ones found in Ireland. Inside, the walls were lined with leather tack and signed photos of famous trainers and jockeys.

The hostess pointed him in the right direction and he quickly made his way to Sean Harris's booth. The journalist sat alone, polishing off his lunch. He was a big man sporting an exaggerated mustache that was as bright red as his hair.

"Sean Harris? The name is Curran McKenna. I'm—"

"McKenna, is it? I know who you are." Harris

wiped his mouth with a napkin, then waved it at the other side of the booth. "Sit. Shall I get you a pint?"

"Nothing for me, but many thanks." He needed to keep a clear head.

Harris took a swig from his own pint of dark brew. "So what can I do for you?"

"I understand you're friends with Gavin Shaw."

"That I am. But I haven't heard from him in some time, not since the fall meet at Keeneland, actually." His tone grew cautious. "Are you thinking of going into a partnership with him?"

"Why would you ask that?"

Harris hesitated, then said, "He was talking about making some changes. I thought you might be part of the picture."

"Any particular reason he was partner-hunting?"

"I get the feeling there's a story here," Harris said, his expression wily. "One that might interest me. And my readers, of course."

"What if I promise to give you a story when I get it all sorted out."

Harris narrowed his gaze on Curran. "You would be square with me?"

"Absolutely. I have no reason not to be."

Other than Jane, Curran thought. But the truth would come out in the end anyway. Better that he have the upper hand on the way the story was written.

Harris nodded in agreement. "It was the money," he said. "Gavin was drowning in debt."

Money—a possible reason for going against one's own grain, Curran thought. "Bad luck at the track?"

"You could say that. But not with the Thoroughbreds he was training. Gavin Shaw has always had a serious problem picking the right horse to bet on.''

"He was a gambler, then.''

"Compulsive. He would lose, then bet again, bigger, thinking he could make up for the first loss. It didn't happen that way, of course. Not often enough, anyway.'' Suddenly Harris went still. "*Was.* You said *was,* not *is.*''

"A slip of the tongue,'' Curran hedged. "So how did Shaw think going into partnership with another trainer would help?''

"Well, he never quite defined it as being another trainer. He was vague. Frankly, I feared he was looking for a less honorable backer. A loan shark.''

"He was that desperate?''

"Though he tried not to show it, I believe so.''

If Shaw had gotten involved with a loan shark, he would have been susceptible to intimidation. Enough to break a horse's legs? Curran figured the odds were good.

"I think you've given me some of the answers for which I've been searching.''

"But what are the questions?'' Harris asked.

"Let me get back to you on that one.''

"I'll take your word on it. Don't let me down.''

With a nod and a shake and a simple thanks, Curran left Harris to mull over the conversation with the remainder of his pint.

The last thing Jane would want was to cooperate with a reporter, Curran knew. But he had no such compunctions. No matter how the relationship between them turned out, he would see that she was safe. That took getting to the truth and he might have to be ruthless to succeed.

Gavin Shaw had obviously found that partner he'd been looking for, one who had pushed him to act against his own nature. And whoever had pushed him to break Finn's legs had undoubtedly killed Timothy Brady because he had been a threat to this mystery partner.

But what kind of threat?

That someone had to be associated with Stonehenge. He was certain of it.

Saladin? Easterling? Phyllis herself?

Whatever the plan, it had somehow backfired, and now Jane's very life was in jeopardy. If only he could figure out what Jane knew that would hurt someone in the industry, he would be able to find the murderer.

HE WAS HALF-RECLINING on her bed waiting for her when Phyllis Singleton-Volmer flew into her suite. Agitated, muttering to herself, she didn't notice him at first. Then, again, she never seemed to notice those below her. Just as she seemed never to get her own hands dirty.

But when she did become aware of him, she went very still and her eyes went wide.

"What are you doing here?"

At least she didn't pretend that she didn't know who he was.

"I wanted to meet the woman pulling the strings face-to-face—the one responsible for everything."

"I think you'd better leave before I call the authorities."

"Call them." He indicated the telephone. "They'll want to hear what I have to say."

Shaking, she sat on the chair at her make-up table. "I don't know what you think you know—"

"Timothy Brady talked...before he died."

"You?"

"Surprised?" He shrugged. "So was I."

"What is it you want from me?"

With a gloved hand, he pulled the gun from under the pillow where he'd found it.

"To let you know that enough is enough."

HER FEELING OF uncertainty growing, Jane paced the length of the house. She couldn't sit around and do nothing, but what choices did she have?

The shrill of the phone scraped her spine.

Fumbling, she picked up the receiver to find the sheriff at the other end.

"Biggs, I thought you were on your way."

"Had a little detour. More bad news. The Single-ton-Volmer woman is dead."

"Dead?" Jane echoed, sitting. "How?"

"Looks like she killed herself rather than face the music. Shot herself in the heart through one of them fancy pillows off her bed."

"You're sure it was suicide?"

"Not officially, not until we check the prints on the gun. We do know the gun was hers, though."

"Dear Lord."

Jane heard the rest through a haze. Something about his having a chat with Mukhtar Saladin and Holt Easterling. *If* he could find them.

Hanging up, Jane wished Curran were there so she could talk to him, tell him about Phyllis, discuss whether Saladin or Easterling was more likely to be her partner in crime, but he was off with that reporter Harris.

As had been the case for the past months, she was drawn to seek out Finn, her partner in emotional pain. Working with the stallion would make her feel better...would relieve her mind, at least for a while.

Convinced of that, she grabbed her cane and set out for the stables.

The farm was exceptionally quiet. Everyone seemed to have gone for lunch at the same time. Not that she minded. Without distraction, she was able to focus on the smells of newly mowed grass and the nickering of mares to their foals.

She was reminded of why she loved Grantham Acres so much. Of why her heart would break if she lost it.

Simply put, the farm was part of her soul.

As was Finn.

They would have their own connection always, Jane thought, as she let him out of his stall and walked shoulder-to-shoulder with him into the paddock, where she set her cane against the fence and put the stallion on a lunge line. If she lost the farm, he would be auctioned off to the highest bidder.

Thinking she would be lost without him, she touched his scarred nose. For once, instead of bobbing his head and pulling away, he pushed the soft velvet into her hand, just the way he had when she'd first bought him.

"That's my lad," she murmured, touching his forehead with hers. "We're a pair, you and I."

She let out the length of the line and began working him. He stretched out his long legs, his chestnut hide gleaming in the afternoon light.

So much beauty almost destroyed, she thought.

Turning in place with the stallion working in a circle around her, Jane closed her eyes for a moment and breathed in deeply. She felt the change first through her fingers when the lunge line went slack.

Immediately she flicked open her eyes. The stallion had set his ears back slightly and his nostrils flared and his flesh quivered. His squeal shot up her spine and made her flesh crawl.

"What is it, Finn?"

Jane sensed the man's presence before she even turned. The bright sun made her blink and squint for a better look as he hopped over the fence and landed in the paddock.

Finn squealed again and pulled the line from her suddenly numb fingers.

It couldn't be...

But there was no mistaking that auburn hair or those green eyes.

"Hello, Jane. Surprised to see me, are you?"

"Gavin! You're alive—"

Her head went light and she swayed. Then she caught herself and mustered all the strength she still possessed as she saw him pull a tire iron from his waistband and she realized the terrible truth.

Gavin Shaw had come to finish what he had started.

He meant to kill her.

Chapter Fifteen

Curran was just leaving Lexington when a wave of unease washed through him.

He tried to ignore the sensation, put it to the stress of his romance with Jane gone sour and him without a clue.

But the feeling nagged at him and he couldn't rid himself of the idea that something was terribly wrong. It was the same sensation that he'd had when Jane had been locked in the curing barn.

Worry erased the bitter memory of their argument and her coolness toward him afterward. He concentrated on Jane, wondering if she would once more block him.

A wave of nausea washed through him...
Curran!

Jarred by the unexpected quickness of the connection and the intensity of Jane's emotions, Curran pulled himself back to the now in time to see that he'd crossed into the oncoming traffic. He swerved to avoid a truck, with only seconds to spare. Then, heart pounding, he pulled his vehicle to the side of the road and threw on the brakes.

"Come on, Jane, what's wrong?" he muttered, focusing inward once more.

Focusing on fear...anguish...despair...
A length of metal in a man's hand...
Heart pumping...stomach knotting...
Curran, please!

It took him a moment to register the sensations. To realize that was no pipe in the man's hand and this wasn't a replay of Hudson Valley. Whatever he was imagining was actually happening now.

Certain that Jane was in trouble and sending him a distress signal, Curran put the car in gear, stepped on the accelerator and took off for the farm like a madman. As he drove, he kept seeing the metal tool in the man's hand—another potential instrument of death.

Jane couldn't die. He loved her. He wouldn't let it happen.

If only he could get there on time...

"WHY, Gavin?" Jane asked as she stared disbelievingly at the man who should be a ghost. "Why did you pretend to be dead? I did nothing but care about you." She wouldn't say she loved him, not even to save her own life, not when she finally knew what love was. "Why did you set me up?"

"I had no choice."

"We all have choices."

"It was my life or Finn's," Gavin said, glancing at the fear-stricken horse with what Jane swore was a look of regret. He turned back to her. "You know what debt is like. But you have Grantham Acres. I had nothing to save me."

"Which I don't understand," she said, keeping her

tone even, to keep him settled. She would run if she could, but of course he had seen to that. "You're a successful trainer."

"But not a successful gambler."

"Gambling debts?" Surely Curran would return any time now, Jane thought. All she had to do was keep Gavin talking. "That's what all this terror has been about?"

"It's been about my not having my legs broken. About my staying alive. I didn't want to do any of it, Jane, I swear to you. I cared for you, I really did. That's why I called you about buying Finn mac Cumhail in the first place. I thought it was a way out of debt for you. And maybe for me, too. But it all went wrong. No sooner did we transfer title than the blackmail started. I thought I could get away with it, that you would never know what I did to Finn. I vowed to stand by you and make it up to you somehow."

Jane stared at him aghast. "You're saying you had feelings for me?"

"I still do...not that it matters anymore. I'm a changed man. Trying to break Finn's legs just about killed me...*you* about killed me."

Oddly, there was no rancor in his voice at the accusation. As if he didn't blame her. Why, then, had he been trying to murder her?

"I thought I *had* killed you," Jane said. "And I didn't know how I was going to live with myself after that."

And she could see that Gavin couldn't live with himself, either. Not with the man he was—a weak man, perhaps, but one with a heart and soul. What he felt he'd been forced into had made him some kind of monster. That he'd been blackmailed didn't excuse him. And yet she remembered his drunken desperation that night in Hudson Valley, and despite everything that had happened since, she almost felt sorry for him. Almost.

"But you did live," Jane said, again trying to call Curran with her mind while she kept Gavin talking. "You survived both a pitchfork and a horrible fall."

"No vital organs involved," Gavin explained. "The water was cold enough to slow the bleeding. And the current carried me to the bank downstream. It took me most of the night to crawl to the closest house. It was locked up, but I broke in to use the telephone."

"To call Tim Brady for help?"

Gavin nodded. "Smart lass. He was the conduit for the whole thing. I never did give you enough credit, Jane. You might have figured out what happened to Finn even if you *hadn't* caught me trying to break his legs."

Recognizing the serious note of regret in his voice, Jane wondered if it was for Finn and her or for himself.

Drawing one last time on her own pain, she asked, "When you murdered Tim, did that nearly kill you, as well?"

Gavin's expression changed subtly. "Not at all." His voice grew cold. "He'd been riding me for months. The person who bought my debt had been using him as a go-between. I got the details, including her name, from Timothy before I evened things up between us."

"Phyllis Singleton-Volmer."

"Aye. The bitch was the marionette mistress and

we were her puppets. When she got wind of our plans for entering Finn mac Cumhail in the Thoroughbred Millions, she was determined that he would not run against Stonehenge. She bought my debt from a loan shark to control me. Only I didn't know it then. Not until I got it out of Timothy before he passed on.''

A way of avoiding the word murdered, Jane thought. ''So you killed Phyllis, too?''

Her pulse began to rush as Gavin stroked the tire iron. Where was Curran? Had she driven him away, severed the connection for good? Surreptitiously, she looked for an escape even as she kept up the dialogue.

''I had to kill her,'' Gavin said. ''She knew too much about me.'' He shook his head and again softened his voice. ''Just as you do.''

Panic was setting in. When Gavin stopped talking, she was done for, Jane reasoned. With her bad knee, there was no escape for her. She couldn't run. Couldn't climb the fence. Couldn't fight a man Gavin's size. She had no weapon. Except…she looked past a nervous Finn to where her cane lay propped against the fence.

''You don't have to kill me, Gavin.'' Jane made herself sound more reasonable than she was feeling. ''I know you don't want to. That's not who you are.''

''Were,'' he quickly corrected her. ''I'm a changed man, Jane. I don't want to kill you, but I must. Now that my debt is paid, I plan on reclaiming my life. And you're the only one who can still stop me.''

''I won't stop you. I promise,'' she lied. ''I can help you, get you money to start over.''

"How, when you have none yourself?"

Jane glanced at Finn, huddled against the fence nearby, his sides heaving. "When Finn wins the Classic Cup, I'll have more than enough," she said. "It was your idea to save Grantham Acres, remember?"

"Aye, and it was a good one…until certain people interfered and made me into what I am. Look at him now. Do you really expect you can even enter him in a claiming race? Classic Cup—don't make me laugh!"

Finn *had* reverted to the way he'd been when she'd first brought him to the farm. He was pawing the ground. Squealing low in his throat. Foaming. His bright chestnut coat had gone dark with sweat.

"Everyone knows this horse is crazy," Gavin said, hitting the tire iron against his open palm. "No one will really be surprised that he killed you. Then he'll be put down. And I can return to Ireland and work as a trainer with my reputation intact."

He was so deluded, Jane realized. Too many people now knew about him. Not that she was about to be specific lest she put someone else in danger.

"The authorities here know that you're supposed to be dead," Jane said instead, carefully backing away from him toward the open barn door. Perhaps if she could get inside… "They know about Tim and Phyllis."

"They think Phyllis committed suicide, and they'll come to the conclusion that she killed Tim to protect herself. I'm afraid they'll never know the whole story, and if they figure it out, it will be too late. There is no extradition treaty between Ireland and the United States."

Gavin quickly stepped toward her and grabbed her arm to stop her from getting away. Even as she struggled to free herself, Jane gave trying to alert Curran one last try. She closed her eyes for a second to focus and sent out a silent cry for help.

Finn's answering scream of fury ripped through her like a knife.

Jane opened her eyes to see him stop pawing the ground and charge Gavin, who let go of her. He raised the tire iron to ward off the stallion. Even as Jane scrambled back, Finn reared on his hind legs.

And even as she had come to his rescue, the stallion now came to hers. Finn struck out with his front hooves and caught Gavin's arm.

Gavin screamed in pain and the tire iron went flying.

And, seemingly out of nowhere, Curran came flying into the fray and knocked Gavin off his feet. Finn leaped over them both, mindlessly racing himself around the perimeter of the paddock.

The two men rolled over one another, sending up a cloud of dust, punching at each other, mostly ineffectively. Gavin's arm might be hurt, but it didn't seem to be broken, Jane noted. He gave as good as he got.

Quaking with relief and the fury that she hadn't yet expressed, Jane pushed herself to the fence and grabbed her cane. She looked to Finn who'd stopped at the other side of the paddock and was whinnying nervously. She held out her hand and whistled softly. Circling the men, the stallion came straight toward her and stood at her side, his flesh trembling.

When Finn allowed her to touch his neck with no

more than a shiver in reaction, Jane whispered words of thanks. All was not lost with the stallion, at least.

But both she and Curran had to come out of this alive.

At the moment, he was her main concern. She breathed a sigh of relief as he landed a punch square to Gavin's jaw and then pinned him to the ground.

"Get out of here, Jane!" he yelled. "Go call Biggs. Now!"

The moment's inattention was a mistake. Her wily former lover had been faking that he'd given up. He suddenly rolled and switched positions. Landing on top of Curran, he backhanded the man she loved, knocking him senseless.

The next thing Jane knew, Gavin had his hands around Curran's throat and was strangling him.

"Gavin, don't!" She cried. "Curran!"

As her focus involuntarily shifted, she gasped.

No breath...black spots swam before her eyes... her vision faded...

Before she herself passed out, Jane forced herself back out of the connection.

She stumbled forward, screaming, "Gavin, stop, please!"

If she didn't do something, Gavin Shaw would kill the man she loved. Then he might as well finish her off.

Pure instinct drove her to raise her cane as a weapon. When she swung, she didn't hold back. The silver horse's head connected with Gavin's and it was *his* head that gave with a visible snap.

His hands left Curran's throat and raised to touch the blood spurting from his temple. He fell to one side, releasing Curran, who lay there like a man already dead.

Looking up at Jane, Gavin whispered, "Now you've gone and killed me," as his eyes fluttered and his body went limp.

Jane ignored the body twisted back on itself and flew to the ground and Curran. Her knee sang but she celebrated the pain. She was alive. And so must he be.

"Curran," she whispered, and felt for a pulse in his neck. She found one. Barely. It was weak and thready.

Continuing to touch him, she concentrated on him, on his spirit, on focusing.

Pain...and then a great sense of emptiness.

Panicking, she pushed back with positive images.

In the grandstand at Churchill Downs, they looked out on Finn mac Cumhail as he crossed the finish line, beating Stonehenge by a neck...

She visualized Curran turning to her, pure happiness lighting his beloved face as she smothered it with kisses.

I love you, Curran, I love you. Stay with me.

Stay with me always...

"That all depends."

The softly croaked words threw her out of the connection. Curran's eyes fluttered open and she could see he was trying to focus on her.

Jane's heart raced as she cradled his face with her hands and asked, "Depends on what?"

"Whether or not you're willing to declare your love to the whole world."

GAVIN WASN'T DEAD, after all—he'd merely suffered some blood loss and a concussion.

Jane was more thankful than she could say. No more guilt. At least there wouldn't be once she'd told Curran the details she'd hidden from him.

She waited until after Biggs had Gavin taken away and had told them that their more detailed accounts of what had gone on could wait until they'd had time to take care of Finn properly and get themselves cleaned up.

The sheriff's car was only halfway down the driveway before she said, "Curran, about me and Maggie Butler—"

"I realize that I wasn't being fair comparing you to her," he interrupted. "Her life wasn't so complicated. And it wasn't on the line."

"But I understand what you were feeling. I was holding back, but you knew about Gavin, didn't you? You thought I had been having an affair with him and hiding it because I was embarrassed that he was someone who worked for me, just as Maggie was embarrassed to let her world know about you."

He nodded. "It all felt so familiar."

"I'm not embarrassed about you, I promise," Jane said. "And I wasn't embarrassed about Gavin, either, at least not when it began." Her mouth went dry as she finally geared herself to tell the whole truth at last. "Gavin charmed me. He wined and dined me and too quickly asked me to marry him."

"A whirlwind courtship."

"He seduced me. I know this sounds odd in this day and age, but I had never been…uh, seduced before. But I had never been in love before, either, and didn't know if I would ever find it. At least not the storybook kind. Gavin Shaw, Irish horse trainer, seemed to be a perfect match for me," she went on. "I was afraid of the responsibility I had taken on. Nani and Susan and Grantham Acres. I was afraid I couldn't do it myself. A family of my own with a man who shared my love of the Thoroughbred industry seemed perfect. A future together seemed perfect."

"You loved him, then."

Curran's flat tone made her stare and wonder what filled his thoughts. Surely he couldn't think that. Surely he knew that if she was his legacy, then he was hers.

"I was attracted to Gavin and to his offer to be a full partner in life," she said honestly. "I did care for him and I thought love was something that merely needed time to grow, as did our relationship."

"And yet you accepted his proposal."

"Yes, I did. I had convinced myself that I was lucky to have found him. And because it was so sudden and I was away from home, I didn't tell anyone. I wanted to wait at least until Nani and Susan met Gavin. Susan had been so upset by Daddy's death, and then Mother's remarrying and moving...I just couldn't make another change without telling her in person."

"And then before you came home, Shaw tried to break Finn's legs. After which, he tried to kill you."

Jane shuddered at the memory.

"These past months, I thought my only saving grace in this whole debacle was that I hadn't brought my most dreadful mistake to light. I had to steel myself to take my neighbors' pity. I couldn't have borne their scorn, as well. Does that make me a terrible person?''

''It makes you wonderfully human.''

''I really didn't know what love was like, Curran, not until you. I distrusted my own feelings when I realized how I felt about you. I thought I was repeating my mistake. I couldn't trust myself.''

''And now?''

''And now I know you're the best thing that ever happened to me. I'm only sorry that I didn't wait for you, that you weren't the one who—''

Before she could finish, Curran hushed her with a kiss. If she had any doubts that he was the right man for her, that sweet, passionate kiss brushed them aside.

''You're mine now,'' Curran said huskily, drawing his lips from hers. ''And that's all that matters. We both had a journey we had to take to find each other. If you hadn't met Shaw...if Finn hadn't been hurt...you wouldn't have needed me.''

''Don't say that. I *do* need you. I'll always need you.''

Curran pulled her close to his heart, ''You have me, then, my Sheena, for the rest of our lives. You are my legacy.''

Jane clung to him, knowing that no matter how things turned out with Finn, they would be all right.

Together.

Epilogue

Curran held on to Jane tightly as the gates opened and twelve powerful Thoroughbreds took the track at the start of the Classic Cup. Finn mac Cumhail had drawn the number-twelve slot and was closing toward the rail at the back of the field.

"Just let him be on the board," Jane murmured.

Curran countered, "Just let him win!"

He knew Jane was grateful that he'd been able to get Finn ready to race in time. But Curran wanted him to win more than anything he'd wanted in his life—other than his Sheena, of course—and not for himself this time, but for Jane and Belle and Susan and for Grantham Acres itself.

"He's blocked," Jane said, sounding dismayed.

Indeed, as the horses came to the first turn, Finn was in the middle of the pack, Stonehenge clearly ahead of him in third behind the pacesetters.

"He's fine," Curran said, hoping he really was. "Jimi will watch for a break."

The young jockey had worked wonders with Finn during their morning workouts at the track.

As the horses thundered down the backstretch, Curran watched through binoculars. Finn was firmly entrenched in sixth, boxed in by an American and a French horse.

"Come on, Finn mac Cumhail," his sister Keelin shouted. "Make your Irish ancestors sing with pride for you!"

Curran grinned at her. Seeing little Kelly in one of Tyler's arms, Keelin pressed against his side with the other, Curran was envious.

Anxious to start his own family, he gave Jane a squeeze as, halfway through the second turn, Jimi broke Finn out of the box by dropping back slightly and bringing him to the outside.

"Come on, Finn!" Jane cried.

The chant went up in their box. "Finn! Finn! Finn!" Granthams and McKennas and Leightons all cheering the stallion on together.

As the horses rounded the last turn and headed for home, Curran saw Finn had a clear shot but wasn't making his move. He focused on the stallion.

The ground came up to meet him as he passed the nearest horse and drew up to Stonehenge.

Blinking, Curran looked out to see it happening.

Stonehenge's jockey used his crop and the English stallion surged forward. But Finn kept with him, and when they passed the horse in the lead, they were neck and neck. The finish line was an eighth of a mile away.

"Finn! Finn! Finn!"

Jane was grabbing at him in her excitement and jumping up and down.

The rival stallions were pulling away from the field.

Finn! Finn! Finn!

The finish line—concentrate!

"He's going to do it!"

Jane's scream shifted Curran's reality as Finn took the lead and crossed the finish line by a neck.

Exactly as Jane had projected to him when he'd lain unconscious in the paddock.

And now she threw her arms around his neck and rained kisses on his face.

"I love you! I love you! I love you!"

"I knew you could do it, boyo," Keelin said, beaming.

"As did I," Belle added.

"You did it!" Susan cried. "You saved Grantham Acres!"

"It was a joint effort," Curran said, his arm possessively around Jane.

Something he repeated to the media a few minutes later when cameras were focused on them and microphones were shoved in their faces.

"Do you agree, Miss Grantham?" a reporter asked.

"Absolutely," Jane said. "And it will continue to be a joint effort, if I have anything to say about it. Curran McKenna and I are a team, in every sense of the word."

"Ah, Sheena…"

Then, on national television—as big an audience as one could get—Jane threw her arms around his neck and kissed him senseless.

* * * * *

THE McKENNA LEGACY

lives on with the June 2002
release of HI #665

COWBOY PROTECTOR

the next installment in Patricia Rosemoor's
thrilling family saga from Harlequin Intrigue

A ROYAL MONARCH'S SEARCH FOR AN HEIR LEADS TO DANGER IN:

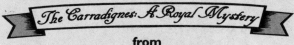

The Carradignes: A Royal Mystery

from
HARLEQUIN®
INTRIGUE®

Plain-Jane royal secretary Ellie Standish wanted one night to shine. But when she was mistaken for a princess and kidnapped by masked henchmen, this dressed-up Cinderella had only one man to turn to—one of her captors: a dispossessed duke who had his own agenda to protect her and who ignited a fire in her soul. Could Ellie trust this man with her life...and her heart?

Don't miss:
THE DUKE'S COVERT MISSION
JULIE MILLER June 2002

And check out these other titles in the series

The Carradignes: American Royalty

available from HARLEQUIN AMERICAN ROMANCE:

THE IMPROPERLY PREGNANT PRINCESS
JACQUELINE DIAMOND March 2002

THE UNLAWFULLY WEDDED PRINCESS
KARA LENNOX April 2002

THE SIMPLY SCANDALOUS PRINCESS
MICHELE DUNAWAY May 2002

And coming in November 2002:
THE INCONVENIENTLY ENGAGED PRINCE
MINDY NEFF

Available at your favorite retail outlet.

HARLEQUIN®
Makes any time special ®

Visit us at www.eHarlequin.com

HICR